**IF YOU M..
THIS BOOK, YO..
BE CHARGED $..**

SPECIAL MESSAGE TO READERS

This book is published under the auspices of

THE ULVERSCROFT FOUNDATION

(registered charity No. 264873 UK)

Established in 1972 to provide funds for research, diagnosis and treatment of eye diseases. Examples of contributions made are: —

A Children's Assessment Unit at Moorfield's Hospital, London.

•

Twin operating theatres at the Western Ophthalmic Hospital, London.

•

A Chair of Ophthalmology at the Royal Australian College of Ophthalmologists.

•

The Ulverscroft Children's Eye Unit at the Great Ormond Street Hospital For Sick Children, London.

You can help further the work of the Foundation by making a donation or leaving a legacy. Every contribution, no matter how small, is received with gratitude. Please write for details to:

THE ULVERSCROFT FOUNDATION,
The Green, Bradgate Road, Anstey,
Leicester LE7 7FU, England.
Telephone: (0116) 236 4325

In Australia write to:
THE ULVERSCROFT FOUNDATION,
c/o The Royal Australian College of Ophthalmologists,
27, Commonwealth Street, Sydney,
N.S.W. 2010.

Fred Pennington was reared on a remote Devon farm, where he worked with his parents to secure a hard-earned living. During those years he learnt duty towards his neighbour, and the value of friendship and loyalty. These experiences convinced him of the Divine purpose of God's will, and he became a parish priest, hypnotherapist and exorcist. He was inspired to use his exceptional skills to perform miracles, healing and helping people with both mental and physical ailments.

THE HUNGRY FORTIES

Fred Pennington's great grandfather was born in 1823 and by 1912 he had become completely blind. He lived with Fred's family on a farm on the west coast of Devon at Hartland. When Fred started school early in the first world-war, his job on coming home was to take him for a walk around the fields. The old man was able to recount events of the past in great detail, and this book is based upon the stories he told Fred during their walks. Born into a humble labourer's family, living for Fred's great grandfather had been a continuous struggle just to have enough to eat and, later, to bring up his family.

Books by Fred Pennington
Published by The House of Ulverscroft:

FROM PLOUGHBOY TO PRIEST

FRED PENNINGTON

THE HUNGRY FORTIES

Complete and Unabridged

ULVERSCROFT
Leicester

First Large Print Edition
published 2000

All rights reserved

> British Library CIP Data
>
> Pennington, Fred *1911* –
> The hungry forties.—Large print ed.—
> Ulverscroft large print series: general fiction
> 1. Large type books
> I. Title
> 823.9′14 [F]
>
> ISBN 0–7089–4210–5

Published by
F. A. Thorpe (Publishing)
Anstey, Leicestershire

Set by Words & Graphics Ltd.
Anstey, Leicestershire
Printed and bound in Great Britain by
T. J. International Ltd., Padstow, Cornwall

This book is printed on acid-free paper

Introduction

My great grandfather was born in 1823 and by 1912 he had become completely blind. He lived with my family on the farm where I was brought up which overlooked the Atlantic Ocean on the west coast of Devon at Hartland. When I started school early in the first world-war, my job on coming home each evening was to take him for a walk around the fields.

It was harvest time when I started to do this and as I firmly grasped the old man's hand to guide him through the stately rows of 'shocks' of corn I can remember a wonderful peace pervading the whole scene. The sun was setting beyond the horizon of the great ocean like a huge ball of fire, its soft rays spreading a shimmering glow upon those mighty waters which stretch for more than 3,000 miles to Nova Scotia in Canada.

The only sounds to disturb that idylic experience were the crackle of stubble under our feet where corn had been cut with scythes and the cawing of the rooks as they made their way home to roost in the great oak trees overlooking the beautiful 12th Century

Abbey just a mile away.

My great grandfather was a very stately figure with a long white beard who walked with a straight back and head held high despite his 92 years. He had a very alert mind and was able to recount events of the past in great detail, but I think I must have often tired him as I bombarded that patient old man with questions about his life in the 19th Century in which I seemed to be so interested.

His early life had been far from easy as was the case for many people in this area at that time. He had been born into a humble labourer's family and living for him had been a continuous struggle just to have enough to eat, enough clothes to keep him warm and, later, to bring up his family decently and honourably.

This had been especially hard during the decade that has come to be known as 'The Hungry Forties'. During that time there were two corn harvest failures followed the next year by a disease that destroyed the whole of the potato crop. It was this latter disaster which caused so much hardship among the population of that area as it did in the West of Ireland at the same time. Potatoes were the mainstay of most peoples diet and were used at almost every meal in some form.

This, combined with the desperate shortage of flour, meant that many people were on the verge of starvation which in turn brought about many serious conditions, especially in children.

This made men go to extreme lengths to provide the necessities for life for their families. One of the more bizarre of such practices was that of 'wrecking' which, although it was carried out in great secrecy, was a common experience for small groups of men during the 1840's. My great grandfather would have been in his twenties at that time and he knew men who had taken part in such practices.

This book is based upon the stories he told me of life in this area during those years.

FRED PENNINGTON

1

'Keep the old mare moving, Jim'. The sound of Harry Hickman's voice was almost instantly lost in the roar of the storm force southwesterly wind sweeping in from the sea.

Jim Foster was leading a horse slowly to and fro along the top of the high cliffs of Hartland on the North Devon coast facing on to the Atlantic Ocean. Firmly fixed on the horse's back was a huge ship's lantern, its paraffin flame at times almost extinguished by the terrible wind. Jim had great difficulty in standing upright; in fact, so great was the force of the storm that he could lean against the wind and it would support the weight of his body. From time to time he needed to hold on to the horse to prevent himself being blown over.

The night was completely dark, without moon or stars, and from time to time lowering clouds brought heavy showers of rain. Not far from Jim and his horse Harry Hickman and three companions huddled together in the lee of some gorse bushes while trying to assess the situation in which they were involved. They were on a wrecking expedition — an experience they had all taken part in many times.

It was high tide at eight o'clock on that wild January night in 1840 as those men peered out into the inky blackness. Huge waves were crashing against the foot of the cliffs a sheer three hundred feet below them, whilst the wind whipped the spume from the crest of the foaming waters, covering the ground around them as with snow.

Those men knew that not many feet below the surface of those raging waves lines of rocks like sharks' teeth stretched out from the cliffs for hundreds of yards into the ocean and that any vessel venturing within that distance was doomed to destruction. They knew, too, that seen from the sea that night the light of the lantern on the horse's back would look like the mast-head light of another ship.

Harry Hickman was employed by Farmer Passmore whose land extended to the cliff edge in that area. He had been repairing a stone hedge in a field that day, from where he could look across the ten miles of water to Lundy Island which lies across the Bristol Channel where it meets the Atlantic Ocean.

The day had begun as it was now ending, with a severe southwesterly gale. This had caused several ships to take shelter in what are known as Lundy Roads — an area of calmer waters on the east side of the island where 450 feet high cliffs give shelter from the Atlantic gales. During the afternoon the wind abated somewhat as it often does in that region, before veering to the westerly and increasing in strength.

Just before darkness fell and Harry had to stop work, he noticed that one of the sheltering vessels was on the move again. He watched her as she entered Harty Race, the stretch of water between Lundy and the mainland. The water here is always troubled, even in Summer, but in a gale such as had been raging that day the area often caused great distress to many ships.

By this time the wind had almost reached storm force and as the little vessel battled through the giant waves and began to meet the full impact of the open sea, Harry realised she was going to be in great trouble. At times she plunged into the depths between two huge waves and remained there so long he thought she must have foundered. But there she was again in the now fast fading light, rising almost perpendicularly on her stern, only to plunge down the other side of the wave and become lost to his view.

As he looked across those raging waters

and began to prepare to go home Harry experienced strange feelings stirring within him. He knew that that ship was probably out of one of the South Wales ports and would be carrying coal — what he and his pals would give to get their hands on some of that precious fuel. He knew, too, that in such atrocious conditions at sea it would not be impossible to entice such a ship on to the terrible rocks which surrounded those cliffs. He had taken part in such enterprises many times and had occasionally been successful.

Those feelings became stronger as he trudged through the muddy fields to his dilapidated cottage, carrying his tools and his dinner bag on his shoulders. By the time he reached home, Harry's mind was made up and any feelings of guilt had been smothered by the thought of his wife and children's suffering through cold and hunger. Of course, he argued within himself, he would not want anyone to lose his life and as always they would do all they could to save the crew of such a vessel.

There had been occasions when all hands had been lost when a ship had been wrecked on those rocks, whether he and his friends had been involved or not. Almost every winter at least one ship would come to such an end. Because many lives were lost in this way and the bodies had become so mutilated among the teeth-like rocks, a portion of the local churchyard was especially set aside for the burial of those who were unidentifiable and was known as 'Stranger's Hill'.

As was his custom, Harry did not tell his wife of his plans when he reached home — the fewer people who knew about it the better. Jane Hickman was a gentle person who never complained about her hard circumstances. She had been born into that way of life and saw it as the norm. Her father had been a farm worker but died at the age of 38 years from the dreaded scourge of tuberculosis or 'decline' as it was known locally and from which one in seven of the population under the age of thirty died. Two of Jane's sisters had died of the same disease while still in their teenage years.

Like her husband, Jane had never been to school and could not read or write. At the age of 11 years she had been 'put out to service' as it was called. This meant that she had been contracted to work in the kitchen of the Abbey or 'Big House' as it was locally known, the home of the Squire and landowner. Here she slaved for 12 to 14 hours each day, with one half day free each week, and was paid one shilling a week plus her food.

Jane had married Harry Hickman at the parish church on 4th April 1830 and had seven children in quick succession, three of whom died before their first birthday. She was a good mother who lived for her children, but could give them only little comfort in the harsh conditions in their cottage. Harry worked long hours on the farm for seven shillings a week, of which he gave Jane six to feed and clothe themselves and four children. The farm worker's pay was even worse before the Poor Law Act came into being in 1834. This fixed the wage at seven shillings after a petition by the married paupers of the parish to have their wages raised to this amount. Previously, workers with no children were paid ten pence for a day of twelve hours; those with one child received one shilling and those with two or more were paid one shilling and one penny per day. Every two weeks some workers were 'sold as cattle in a sale to the highest bidder' — some for six pence and some for nine pence a day — the remainder of the wages being paid by the Overseer of the Poor.

Before the crop failures the family's diet, although meagre, was nourishing. Jane's training in the kitchen of the big house was put to good use as she tried to make the most of the little available to her. Like most kitchen Harry would jokingly remark that it was the third time that wood had kept him warm — the first two being when he cut it off the hedge and when he cut up the logs.

The floor of Jane's kitchen was made of hard beaten earth and covered with straw that was renewed weekly. The sitting room or parlour as it was called was a little more comfortable, having sheepskin rugs on the floor. This room was rarely used, except when neighbours visited on a Sunday evening and so had a very damp and musty atmosphere.

There was little comfort in the two tiny bedrooms where some of the children slept on the floor, covered with homemade patchwork quilts and hessian sacks that had been cut open to form blankets. The whole house was very cold and draughty in the winter and when the children went to bed up the rickety staircase their candles were often blown out.

Jane had one great fear in her life which was that she may again become pregnant. Harry was very fond of his beer and often on a Saturday evening he would walk into the little hamlet of Stoke, a distance of some two miles, where he would spend his shilling at the rate of two pence per pint at the Bear Inn. By the end of the farm workers her husband tried to fatten a pig for their own use each year, mainly on potatoes which he grew on the farm where he worked and which, together with one pint of milk each day was regarded as the normal perks for each worker. By the time the pig was fat enough to be slaughtered it had often become so tough as to be far from palatable. Any other meat was a luxury unknown to the Hickman family. The very fat joints of pork would have salt rubbed into them and they were then kept in brine until needed for the table. This, together with fried potatoes was the family's main diet.

Jane did all her cooking in a clay oven which was built into the side of a huge open fireplace. It was heated by wood, the ashes of which were raked out when the oven became hot, and the dishes placed inside. The main fire was the only means of heating in the house and during the winter it was kept alight day and night by means of a huge log known as a 'back stick'. There was a plentiful supply of firewood but it was only obtained by very hard work. Farmer Passmore would give Harry permission to cut down the wood on a certain hedge for his own use but, in return, he would be expected to build up the bank and make it stockproof in his own time. So by the time he sat by the fire in his evening he would be in no fit state to walk home alone and had to be helped by his friends. On such occasions Jane sought refuge in her children's bedroom rather than face her husband's amorous attentions and the inevitable outcome, even though it often resulted in a terrible row.

2

Harry was unusually quiet as they ate their frugle meal that evening after coming home from work. On one or two occasions Jane's eyes met those of her husband and she instinctively knew that something unusual was on his mind. Before she and the children had finished their meal, Harry had put on a hessian sack around his shoulders and another around his waist like an apron and had rushed out of the house without a word to anyone. He knew that if his plan to entice a ship on to those rocks was to succeed he would have to act fast. So he went first to Jim Foster whom he knew would co-operate by bringing his horse to which would be strapped the ship's lantern; then to three other friends who normally made up the team, all of whom lived a short distance from his cottage. These men were sworn to secrecy and Harry trusted them implicitly but he knew the risks involved.

It was not long before they were in their waiting positions in the teeth of a storm which was much worse than they had expected. During this time Harry's thoughts turned to the little vessel he had seen in such difficulties as he was leaving work that evening and he wondered if she was still afloat. That ship was the coaster 'Abervale' which had sailed from Barry in South Wales bound for Falmouth with a cargo of coal. Almost without warning a terrible southwesterly gale sprang up as she sailed down the Bristol Channel, causing Captain Evans to bring his ship into the shelter of Lundy Roads. Here he lay at anchor, along with several other ships all that day, but as the light began to fade, the force of the wind seemed to drop a little, so he decided to continue his voyage. But by the time he had brought 'Abervale' into the open water between Lundy and the mainland, the wind had veered and built up to storm force.

It was too late to turn back, the captain could only keep his ship head-on into the wind and hopefully succeed in riding out the storm. Captain Evans had travelled that route many times, but never before had he seen such heavy seas. In a short while it was completely dark and the mast-head light seemed to be on the point of being extinguished as the ship rolled and pitched in those terrible seas. Although they seemed to be head on into the wind, the skipper was very concerned that they may be drifting on the tide which still had almost one hour before reaching its height. In that comparitively narrow area of sea, there being only ten miles between land points, there would be little room to manoeuvre in such terrible conditions with the wind and tide against them.

George Arnold, the first mate, was even more concerned about their situation than his captain seemed to be. He had lived on that part of the coast for a while and had seen what could happen to a ship that was unfortunate enough to be wrecked in such a storm. At the first opportunity he expressed his thoughts to his captain who seemed grateful to share his own fears with his mate. As they stared out from the bridge into the unbroken blackness of the night, one on either side of the coxwain who was struggling to keep the little ship into the wind, the thought that they may be fighting against impossible odds was in the forefront of their minds.

The weather was getting worse as the minutes passed, the noise of the wind reaching a crescendo in the superstructure of the vessel and the seas became more terrifying. At one point the ship would be in such a deep trough between two waves that it seemed impossible that she would ever get out again. The next minute she would be on the crest of a wave with her propeller out of the water and racing at great speed, before plunging down, at a very steep angle, into another trough.

Captain Evans had every confidence in his ship: she was strong, well built and by no means an old vessel, but he knew there was a limit to how long the engine could hold out under such conditions. Each time the propeller came out of the water there was a risk to the engine bearings. The thought had hardly crossed his mind when a message came up from the engineer reporting that the propeller had been damaged and was virtually out of action. Almost at the same time the forward look-out struggled to get a message to his skipper that he had seen a light on the port beam. The captain could not believe that this was correct: he did not think they had travelled far enough for another vessel to be between them and the coast to the south. But, yes, there it was. He saw it himself — just a momentary flicker before disappearing into the intense darkness. A few minutes later they saw it again and the captain was convinced they were seeing the mast-head light of another vessel. But what could they do? In such mountainous seas it would be impossible to make contact, let alone transfer to her.

At this point George Arnold heard a sound with which he was very familiar. It seemed to him that above the roar of the wind and the crashing of the waves over the ship, he could hear what seemed to be the sound of waves breaking against rocks. He mentioned this to his skipper who thought the mate must have been deceived by the noise of the storm and he ordered the coxwain to change course in order to get a little nearer to the other ship. Hardly had 'Abervale' begun to drift to port when everyone watching realised the frightening reality of what was facing them. There, without any doubt, they could see occasional glimpses of what they knew to be foam from waves breaking upon rocks and, beyond that, they caught a brief glance of towering cliffs.

The three men were speechless: they seemed to have become paralysed. Then Captain Evans ordered everyone up from below decks and they hung on to the bridge rail, waiting for the crash they knew to be inevitable. They knew, too, that their chance of survival was very slim in such conditions but there was no time to discuss the sighting of the light of the other vessel. George Arnold alone had the answer. He had heard of wreckers when he lived in that area, but like so many others, had not believed the rumours.

3

Back on the cliffs, Harry Hickman and his friends struggled to keep their balance in the atrocious conditions which became even worse when the wind veered to the west and they lost their shelter. As always at this point in their plan, Harry's better nature seemed to intrude. Why was he doing this awful thing? Should he pull out even at this late stage? Then, as if in answer to his questioning, a momentary glimmer of light appeared, just a speck in the vast darkness of that terrible night. But the warning was enough to make Harry act quickly. He struggled up to where Jim Foster was holding on to his horse and ordered him to take her home at once. This Jim did without hesitation — he had never been very keen on these escapades and on two or three occasions had made some sort of excuse not to take part. He remembered, too, how his brother had been killed while scrambling down those cliffs on such a night.

Harry Hickman and his three companions knew they had to leave that spot quickly in case someone came that way, although that was most unlikely on such a night. The tide had turned by this time, but still crashing against the foot of the cliffs, but these men knew that by the time they reached the bottom it would have ebbed sufficiently to allow them to stand on the beach. The path down the cliff was well known to them but, under those circumstances, it was a dangerous trek which had to be undertaken with great care. One false step, a loose grip on a wet and slippery rockface, and nothing would save them from crashing to the bottom. As always in such conditions, the wind as it hit the cliff face rushed upwards at almost double its speed at sea level and so made their journey even more difficult.

They eventually reached the bottom safely and began an agonizing wait. Harry's sense of guilt now seemed to impress itself upon him still more deeply and touched him to the very depths of his being. But there was no turning back now — what they had done they had done — they must now do all they could to save those men whose lives they had endangered. They had occasional glimpses of the masthead light of the doomed vessel against the blackness of the heavy clouds and judged that she was still afloat but drifting ever nearer those rocks where, in such a storm, there would be no hope of her surviving. For Harry Hickman the minutes seemed like hours. Would this soul destroying experience never end? He had not felt such intense emotion on any of his previous escapades: it was as if there was a voice within him saying 'Harry, why are you doing this awful thing?' Little did he know that back home in his little cottage his wife Jane was praying for his safety, not knowing where he was or what he was doing.

The intense blackness of the night at last began to lessen a little and a glimmer of light appeared as the heavy clouds began to lift. From their position on the beach Harry and his companions could see the huge waves crashing on to the rocks a little further out to sea, but because of the thick spray could not see the vessel very clearly.

Conversation was still impossible above the combined roar of wind and sea and all they could do was to wait. Harry wondered what was going on in the minds of his friends — they looked calm and relaxed enough but were they agonizing inwardly as he was? Suddenly there was no time for thinking about such things. Above the terrible roar that filled their ears there came another sound — a crashing, splintering sound as of wood being torn apart. The four men looked at each other as their thoughts became as one. They knew that it was the sound of a ship breaking up on those jagged rocks from which no vessel had been known to survive.

Instantly they sprang into action. Their instinct was, as always, to save life. The crashing sound they had heard seemed to have come a little further north from where they were standing. They raced along the narrow strip of beach that was by now clear of the tide, to some higher rocks, the tops of which were becoming visible as the tide receded.

Harry took the lead as they clambered up the slippery sides and, getting soaked from time to time as extra large waves swept over them, they clung on and, keeping as close together as possible, they peered seaward through the darkness. The sight that met their eyes was one of utter destruction. Hardened as they were to such scenes they had never seen a vessel come to its end so quickly. It seemed to them that she had been swept broadside on to the rocks and had been immediately split into two parts — such was the force of wind and sea and this is exactly what had happened. Just before the impact Captain Evans and his crew were huddled together on the bridge of his ship, knowing that they had very little time in which to take any action; in fact, each man knew there was little that could be done. To try to launch a boat into that raging sea would be an act of madness. Their worst fears were realised when, without warning, a massive wave caught the vessel to starboard of the bow and slewed her broadside on into the foaming waters.

'Abervale' was heavily laden and lying low in the water; at the mercy of the jagged ironstone rocks just below the surface. The inevitable crash came even before the crew had time to take the necessary precautions. Some were thrown into the sea as she heeled over and began to break up immediately. Captain Evans and George Arnold clung desperately to the rail of the bridge which was by this time almost constantly under water. Communication was impossible, each man was left to fend for himself as best he could and each knew that if he was forced to let go of that rail his chance of survival amongst those knife-edged rocks would be very slim.

Battered and soaked by the breaking waves it was not long before their strength began to weaken. To add to their problems, the temperature began to drop as the wind veered still further, bringing violent hailstorms. Captain Evans, the elder of the two men, could hold on no longer and George Arnold, realising that his captain's condition was deteriorating, edged a little nearer to him with great difficulty, in order to support him with one hand while holding on to what was left of the bridge rail with the other. But no sooner had George got into position and, as if from nowhere, a massive wave struck the stern portion of the vessel on which they were standing, causing it to lurch forward and throwing both men into the sea.

By this time Harry Hickman had climbed along the raze of rocks as far as he dared, all the while risking his life as wave after wave almost washed him off. After struggling for fifty yards or so he stopped to recover his breath and to wait for his friends to come up to him. They huddled together to decide what to do next while having great difficulty in hearing each other's voices. All thoughts of reward for their night's work had long since disappeared from their minds and they had just one aim now — to save the lives of as many of the crew as they possibly could.

After the wind had veered and between the hail showers, the light had improved still further so that the watchers on the rock could see the wreck of the ship which was nearer to them than they at first thought. In silence they gazed at the result of their terrible act.

Harry seemed to be getting more upset — he was on edge as if he wanted to get out to the vessel to see if anyone remained on board. As they peered seaward in the improving visibility they thought they could see what appeared to be two people standing on the superstructure of what remained of the ship. These sightings were only possible between each wave as it roared over the stricken wreck. At one point it seemed as if one man had been swept away, but no, they were still there but close together now.

Harry could contain himself no longer and made a move as to continue his dangerous climb across the rocks. But his companions could see what he, in his distress, had failed to see — a monstrous wave building up as they often do in such a storm. As it crashed on to what remained of 'Abervale' the men turned their eyes away and clung to the big rock, knowing that their very lives depended on their being able to hold tight enough to prevent themselves being washed off. They knew that no-one on the ship could survive the power of that wave and, when they looked again, the bridge had gone and there was no sign of the two men.

This was too much for Harry — he could stand the strain no longer and decided to swim out to what was left of the ship, even though his friends did their utmost to persuade him that he had no hope of reaching her. They even tried to restrain him physically. Alongside the rocks to which they were clinging there was a narrow channel of sand where children often paddled and swam in more congenial conditions in summer time. Harry took off his boots and jacket and plunged into this channel where the water appeared to be less broken and struck out towards the wreck. He was a strong swimmer, having spent his life beside the sea, but he made little headway because the speed of the waves was increased by the narrowness of the channel between the rocks. Driftwood and even large timbers, which had already broken away from the ship, all helped to impede his progress. He soon became exhausted and was on the point of giving up when a shout from his companions gave him added strength, for there, within a few yards of him, was a man floating face down in the water. No time was lost in getting him back to the beach beyond the reach of the waves, where all four men tried to revive him; but without result. He appeared to have hit his head on a rock as well as having been cut about the face and body.

It was a great disappointment to the rescuers that they had been unable to save this man. Now they had to direct their attention to look for others who may still be alive. Little did they know what heartbreak the next few minutes would bring to them.

They spread out now in order to cover a wider area in their search for other victims. Harry Hickman was, by this time, not only physically exhausted but mentally disturbed. The events of the evening weighed in on him so much that he felt responsible for all that had happened. His mind went back to the afternoon when he was working in the field near the cliffs. Why had he been such a fool as to get involved in an affair like this and, even worse, to involve his friends? There was one consoling thought for him: many ships did end in this tragic way in such a terrible storm, so perhaps the crew of this ship had not seen their light after all.

Harry felt a little more at ease in his mind now, but he had not long to wait for the next act in the drama of that wild January night. Again the cry went up 'Here he is!'. One of the men on the other side of the rock had seen a man in the water. Instantly Harry struggled to the top and, without looking where he was treading, started to rush down the other side but he slipped on the wet seaweed covering the rock and crashed headlong into the water alongside the floating body. The three who watched were shattered but instantly started a rescue operation. Two of them went to help Harry because he was a very heavy man, while the third went to the aid of the survivor from the wreck who was fortunately floating face upward.

Luckily the tide had by this time receded considerably so that they had not far to carry the unfortunate victims before starting to resuscitate them. The man from the wrecked vessel was the first to respond — he was not too badly injured, having only cuts on his face and the effects of having taken in a lot of sea water. His rescuer worked well on him and soon had him fit to sit in the lee of a large rock while he went to help his friends revive Harry. Here he found a more daunting task — Harry had received a heavy blow on the head when he slipped off that rock and he was unconscious. They were just about to give up trying to revive him when he opened his eyes, tried to lift his head and looked at each man individually. His eyes finally rested on the man who had been rescued from the ship and, in a voice so unlike his own, he quietly said 'I'm sorry friend'. He then closed his eyes and fell back dead.

A deep silence settled over that group of men; even the wind seemed to drop from storm force in a short space of time. They were too stunned to take any action. Then George Arnold, for it was he, the mate of the 'Abervale' who had been rescued and revived, asked in a husky voice 'What did that man mean?' There was no answer, but George, confused and exhausted as he was, remembered his suspicions while on board, when he and his captain had seen a light which they at first thought to be the mast-head light of another ship. His question spurred the other men into action. They had to get him food and warm clothing immediately because his condition would soon begin to deteriorate.

Less than half a mile along the beach to the south there was a little harbour called 'The Quay' with a small hotel kept by Mr and Mrs Frank Hockin and some cottages. Here they knew they could get help for this man and themselves, for they were all very wet and cold; so the three men took it in turns to carry him on their backs. Not a word was spoken as they struggled in the darkness to avoid tripping over small rocks or falling into pools of water left by the outgoing tide. Before they reached the houses they realised that George had again lapsed into unconsciousness, which made them hurry still more.

It was now almost two o'clock in the morning and Harry's friends knew that his wife, Jane, would be desperately anxious to know what had kept him so late. They decided that one of them should go to her cottage and break the sad news, while the others roused Frank Hockin. They knew, too, that Frank's wife would be able to give professional help to the unconscious man. They had to cope with the problem of bringing the two bodies away from the beach before the next tide came in.

The elder of the three men, David Kellaway, was a cousin of Jane Hickman so he agreed to go to her as soon as George Arnold was safely in Mrs Hockin's care. So he set off for her isolated cottage, cold and wet as he was, up the steep cliff road and along the narrow twisting lanes for nearly two miles in the darkness. David Kellaway was a morose type of man who was rarely moved by anyone's misfortune; in fact, up to the time of Harry's death, he had shown no emotion whatever. Now he was even less communicative and felt a terrible fear enveloping him: he wished he could run away from it all. As he approached the cottage he saw a candle flickering in the window so he braced himself for the ordeal of having to tell Jane that Harry was dead.

4

After her husband left her and the children in such a hurry during their meal that evening Jane instinctively knew that he had something on his mind. He had acted like this on several occasions, but had never talked to her about what he had been doing when he came home later. He always seemed to find a great many things on the beach the following day, which were very acceptable to them — coal and food as well as plenty of firewood, all of which made life so much more tolerable for the whole family in the harsh conditions in which they lived.

When Jane had put the children to bed that evening she sat by the fire to try and think things out. She determined to have a serious talk with her husband when he came home. She felt that he was hiding something from her, but she would have to choose the right time: she was frightened to question him too closely. She was getting cold by this time — the terrible gale was screaming through the cracks in the badly fitting door and window, driving what little heat there was up the huge open chimney, so she fetched a sheepskin rug from the parlour to wrap around her legs. As she sat staring into what was left of the fire she recalled other such winter evenings when Harry had gone out in the same sort of mood — so unlike his attitude when he was going to the Bear Inn with his friends on a Saturday evening.

As the evening wore on it occurred to Jane that there was a pattern attached to her husband's actions on these particular nights. There was always a heavy gale blowing and he was invariably much later coming home. It was now past two o'clock, she had not known him to be so late as this; Jane began to worry as to his safety in walking home on such a stormy night. Perhaps a branch of a tree had fallen on him as he walked through the woods to their cottage. Should she go and look for him? Getting up from her chair she paced the room to and fro for several minutes. She at last decided there would be no hope of finding him in such complete darkness and, besides, she could not leave the children alone. She peered out of the window on the sill of which stood a little oil lamp, but beyond the tiny area of light which it reflected on the ground outside there was only the blackness of the night.

Jane had just got back to her chair, when she heard a noise outside the door. A stray dog, she thought, or a fox in search of scraps of food or, maybe, it was just the gale blowing things about. But no, there it was again: a cold shiver ran through Jane's spine. Almost immediately there was a tap on the door. She became stiff with fear: whoever could be coming to her house at that time of the night? It certainly was not Harry; he would have walked straight in. At once she was overwhelmed by a feeling that something had happened to her husband.

She picked up the little lamp from the window sill and, shielding the chimney from the draught with her hand, she went to the door intending to open it but was much too frightened. All she could do was to utter a nervous 'come in'. The door opened, slowing on its creaking hinges and, in the dim light of Jane's lamp, a face appeared with a cap pulled so tightly down over it as to make it unrecognisable to her. Then she realised that it was her cousin David who stepped almost hesitatingly over the threshold. Now she knew that her worst fears had become a reality and that something serious had happened to Harry.

David Kellaway was cold and very wet — almost at the point of collapse. Jane quickly got him to the fire and made him change his clothes and put on some of

Harry's, while she made him a hot drink. He made no effort to tell her why he was there. It was as if he had lost all feeling and there was a strange look in his eyes. Then Jane looked straight at him — she could wait no longer, the suspense for her was terrible. 'What's happened, David?' she said in a voice which shook with emotion. But he could only mutter 'He's dead' and broke down and wept. It seemed to Jane that she had been prepared for those words; all she felt was a complete numbness, so that there were no tears.

It was some time before David recovered sufficiently to be able to tell Jane about Harry's death. The story he gave her was that her husband had died while trying to save a seaman from a vessel that had broken up on the rocks in the storm. He made no mention of why they were there at that particular time, neither did Jane seem to have any doubts; she was too shocked.

David Kellaway had casually mentioned the name of George Arnold as the man whom Harry was trying to save, whilst relating the events of that night. At the time, along with many other details, it meant little to her. It was not until later that she remembered the name which seemed to revive a memory of her childhood days, when she had known a man of that name who was a few years older than herself. He had lived not far from her home but she thought the reason she remembered the name was because it was an uncommon one in that area.

As soon as he had recovered, David set off for his home: he knew that his mother, with whom he lived, would be terribly worried as to why he was so late. But Jane could do nothing but continue to be alone with her thoughts. She did not wish to disturb the children at that hour — she was much too numbed to do anything. After she had relaxed a while the inevitable happened — she burst into tears and wept and wept. She felt much more able to cope now and as the first signs of dawn began to show in the stormy sky she prepared herself for the heart-breaking task of telling her children that their father was dead. She knew that her daughter, who was almost ten years old, would be especially hurt. She adored her father and spent a great deal of time with him on the farm during the summer months.

Jane spent the morning of that day comforting her children and after giving them their dinner she felt she just had to talk to someone outside the family — there were so many things to discuss. The idea of going up to the farm to see Mrs Passmore seemed right to her — she and Farmer Passmore had always been kind to her family and ready to help Harry and herself when there had been any trouble, as when their babies had died. Now the need was even greater: the breadwinner of the family had gone. They had only the bare necessities of life, but Jane was thankful she had managed to keep out of debt. But now, how would she keep herself and the children? She was determined not to 'live off the parish', as it was called when poor people were supported by the local authority. It was humiliating enough for her to accept the fact that Harry would have to have a pauper's funeral. She would gladly take in washing, or even go back to work in the big house for a few hours each day if they would have her.

All these thoughts went through Jane's mind as she walked up the wet and muddy lane leading to the farm. As she reached the farmyard gate she suddenly felt overwhelmed by the thought of how she could bring herself to tell the Passmores the terrible news. She met Farmer Passmore in the yard where he was feeding his cattle. One glance at her face told him that something was wrong.

'What's the matter, Jane?' he asked, 'you look so ill'. Then she burst into tears and, between her sobs, she could only whisper 'Harry is dead'.

James Passmore was clearly shocked to learn of the death of his workman who had served him faithfully for so long and he was lost for words except to say in a voice he hardly recognised as his own 'I can't believe its true, I'm so sorry'. After recovering his composure he said 'Come in and talk to my wife'.

He took Jane into his large kitchen where Mrs Passmore was equally shocked but she sought to comfort Jane and made her a cup of tea. After a while Jane was able to tell them what had happened and her concern for the future. Farmer Passmore then left the two women alone while he tried to work things out in his mind as to what he could do to help. When he returned he found Jane to be much more relaxed and was able to give her the plan he had arranged. He would make all the arrangements for the funeral as well as cover the cost. If Jane could arrange for the children to be looked after for a few hours each day he would employ her to help his wife in the house.

This offer was gratefully accepted by Jane and it brought a further flood of tears, much to her embarrassment. But there was another problem that was secretly worrying her. The cottage in which she lived was a 'tied house' which meant that when her husband ceased to work for Farmer Passmore she would have to move out in order that he could have another workman. But where could she find another house? She mentioned this to him as she was leaving and he assured her that it would not have to happen for some time. He promised her that he would do all he could to help and that she was not to worry about it.

As Jane walked home to her cottage she felt relieved and grateful to the Passmores for the help she had been promised. Now she had to face up to the present and the heartache of the funeral. She wished her husband's body to be brought back to the cottage and rested in the little parlour until the burial. She talked to her cousin David about this but he did not think it was a good idea. He said there would have to be an inquest and it might be several days before the funeral could take place. David suggested that it would be better if Harry's body was taken to the mortuary adjoining the parish church where the burial would take place.

The inquests were duly held and David Kellaway identified the body of Harry Hickman in order to spare additional pressure being put upon his widow. George

Arnold did the same for his captain, Mervyn Evans, since he was the only person who knew him there. This was followed two days later by the funeral — a devastating experience for Jane, who took her eldest child with her. As was the custom she, along with all other women present, were heavily draped in black — their veils being kept especially for such occasions. Jane's had been handed down to her by her mother. Funerals at that time were occasions of great solemnity: the men all wearing bowler hats — some of which were green with age.

It was a great relief to the friends of Harry Hickman, who had been with him on the wrecking expedition, that the body of Captain Evans was being taken back to Wales for burial rather than being interred alongside the one who had helped to bring about his death. They were hard young men with very little feeling for another's misfortune, but this latest episode had touched them deeply. They were even too ashamed to discuss the details in each other's company, but resolved that never again would they become involved in such an evil practice.

5

During this time George Arnold had been slowly recovering from his ordeal and preparing to return to his home in Wales. But all the while the events of that terrible night had been foremost in his mind as he tried to find an explanation. Had his ship been carried to her destruction because her captain had seen a light which came from another vessel or — and here George could hardly bring himself to think about it — had his captain been mistaken and had the ship been lured on to those rocks by someone deliberately using a false light?

He had no evidence but it seemed to him to be very strange that those men should have been at the scene of the wreck so quickly. They certainly had no lantern with them — nor anything else which indicated that they had been involved in such an affair. Then George remembered Harry Hickman's words as he died. Had they any link with what had happened? He had not seen those men since that night; in fact he had been in such a shocked state, he doubted if he would remember them anyway.

Because he was unable to attend the funeral of the man who had lost his life in trying to save him, he felt he would like to meet the widow and express his thanks to her. So, on the day before he was due to return home, he asked Frank Hockin to direct him to Jane's cottage. As he walked through the lovely woods it seemed as if he had dreamed all the events of that horrible night. Now it was a beautiful day — the pale winter sun was flickering through the bare boughs of the trees which swayed in the gentle breeze.

He was passing the Abbey, now, which had been a monastery for 400 years from 1160 and he stopped to admire that beautiful building. The only sounds to reach him were the occasional cawing of the rooks high up above him in the lovely old oak trees and the distant croak of a wood-pigeon calling to its mate on the other side of the steep wooded valley. The happenings of that night seemed so far away and so different to the peace he was experiencing now. George would not have called himself a religious man in any sense, but as he strolled along that path it seemed as if he was enfolded in a presence beyond his understanding. A deep sense of gratitude filled his heart which he longed to express in some way.

sadness in her face, and her eyes looked tired and expressionless. Inside the house he could see the results of the deep distress of past days. It was untidy and uncleaned and the children looked grubby and unkempt.

Jane was ill at ease as she offered George a chair while she sat on another with a child on her lap. He, too, hardly knew where to begin the conversation, not wishing to upset her. George explained the reason for his visit — how he felt he could not go back to his home in Wales without first meeting the wife of the man who had died trying to save him from drowning. Jane listened to his story with increasing interest, the details of which she had not heard before. Of course he did not even hint at the suspicions which hovered at the back of his mind — not even telling her of her husband's dying words. For her part Jane felt that she now had the answer to her longstanding query as to why Harry had often been so late in getting home on stormy nights and in her innocence felt as if a great weight had been lifted from her mind.

As Jane listened to her visitor it was as if she was in the company of someone she had known for a long time. Was he the man whose name she vaguely remembered from her childhood? She felt too embarrassed to

As George turned a corner in the [road]
he saw the tall chimney of a house ri[sing]
above the hedge, with a column of [blue]
smoke curling up into the clear cool [air.]
Some twenty or so yards nearer to [him]
the figure of a woman was stooping [over]
a well by the side of the road, pulling
a bucket of water with a rope. She did [not]
notice him approaching, so he had tim[e to]
observe a rather thin, youthful figure [with]
dishevelled hair and poorly dressed, we[aring]
an apron made out of a hessian sack ar[ound]
her waist.

'Oh!' she exclaimed, giving a nervous [start]
as he came up alongside her. 'I w[asn't]
expecting to see anyone yer,' she sa[id in]
her broad Devon dialect.

'Sorry if I frightened you,' said G[eorge.]
'I'm George Arnold. I just wanted y[ou to]
know how sad I am at your husband's [death.]'
He paused a moment, not knowing how [she]
would react.

'Thank you,' replied Jane in a voic[e that]
was almost a whisper. 'Please to come [in for]
a minute'.

'Thanks, I'd like to,' said Georg[e. 'I'll]
carry the bucket of water,' and they [made]
their way into the cottage.

George had no doubts about the i[dentity]
of the young woman. He could see [that]

ask about any details of his life. George, for his part, had no such memories of her or her family, but he was being strangely drawn to her as if by some invisible cord. He attributed these feelings to his desire to comfort Jane in her bereavement and after she had told him of her plans for the immediate future he felt assured that she would be cared for.

George then rose from his chair and, taking her clammy little hand in his, he said 'I am afraid I must go now Jane. You don't mind me calling you Jane do you?'

'Course not,' she shyly replied, for a strange man to use her christian name was a little embarrassing.

'I hope all goes well for you,' he went on. 'Perhaps we shall meet again one day. Goodbye'. As he spoke he looked into her eyes and realised there was a peace there he had not seen when they first met. For this he was thankful and felt that his visit had been worthwhile.

6

George Arnold was 45 years old — a bachelor who had been travelling the seas for 25 years, mainly on coasters out of the South Wales ports carrying coal. He had left North Devon at the age of 20 as many young men did at that time during the agricultural depression in the early years of the 19th century. Because he had been brought up by the sea he naturally turned in that direction to seek a living and he had been satisfied with his choice — arduous and dangerous though it was. He lived from day to day without too much concern for the things of tomorrow, with a kind of bovine contentment that was the envy of his friends.

As he travelled back to Wales from the scene of the shipwreck, George constantly turned over in his mind all that had happened to him and his shipmates after leaving the shelter of Lundy Roads on that fateful night. His life would never be quite the same again. He knew that he had to make a vital decision eventually, either to accept the fact that he might have made a mistake in thinking he had seen a light at all which, he argued, was not impossible in those terrible conditions — and, in this case, he could hold nothing against those men and he could not take up a case against them because he had no real evidence. He did not even know who they were, apart from the man who had died.

But over and above all these thoughts there was one that seemed to take precedence — one that seemed to barge in and push all others to one side — the thought of that young woman without a husband and breadwinner, living with four children in that out-of-the-way little cottage on that wild coast. Would his actions affect her? As the days and weeks of that winter passed George became more and more convinced that he must do nothing that might hurt her.

Back in his bachelor home George soon began to make preparations for his return to the sea. It was the only way of life he knew and he loved it. He signed on again with his old company and within a few weeks he found himself about to leave Barry on board a sister ship to the ill-fated 'Abervale' and, as before, bound for Falmouth. It was to be a sentimental trip for George with all the memories of the previous voyage still so vivid and raw. They came through Harty Race in the late afternoon of that first day out. As they rounded the Point the sun was sinking low in a clear sky, its rays giving a beautiful pink tint to the cliffs and houses along the length of that coast and rising above everything else was the huge tower of the parish church which he remembered passing when he left the Quay, where he had been so well looked after by Frank Hockin and his wife.

George came up on deck just as they came abreast of the spot where 'Abervale' had gone ashore and it seemed to him that all that had happened on that fateful night could not really have taken place at all. As he gazed towards those cliffs, the faces of his shipmates on that voyage seemed to appear to him one by one. He could hear again the voice of his captain shouting above the roar of the storm that he had seen the light of another vessel and his command to his coxwain to change course. Then it seemed as if he was again clinging to the bridge rail trying to support his friend. Finally he was reliving the moment when he looked into Harry Hickman's eyes and heard again the words which seemed at the time to be an apology before they closed in death.

But above all these dreamlike thoughts there was one that was different — one that rose above all the others in George's mind on that beautiful evening as they glided past the scene of former desolation and death. It was the memory of his visit to Jane's home. He could not see that house from his ship but he knew that tucked away in that sheltered valley, among the trees and only some five miles from him, was a little dilapidated cottage where lived a very unhappy and lonely young woman who had, in some strange way, changed his life.

Never before had George given much thought to a member of the opposite sex; he had always felt that women were not for him and he was uncomfortable in their company. But now, here he was, reliving that meeting with Jane and almost wishing he could go ashore and talk with her again. Was it because he felt sorry for her, he wondered, or was there a deeper and more sinister reason which he hardly dared to contemplate — that he might be falling in love with her? The thought almost startled him and he at once turned his mind to the fact that he was due on watch in half an hour. The sun, like a flaming ball, had almost disappeared below the horizon, casting its last rays upon the landscape laid out before him. Minute by minute the view became more indistinct as his ship headed out into the Atlantic ocean and darkness settled upon the scene.

George Arnold was a very withdrawn man

during the whole of that voyage. He knew several of the crew quite well but felt that he could not confide in any of them. He knew how they would react. Old bachelor Arnold getting himself interested in women. Surely not. He knew how his friends would make fun of it at his expense. Even he, himself, could not understand exactly what was happening to him so he tried to put the matter out of his mind and get on with the job he had to do.

Jane had not been so immediately influenced by her meeting with George. She remembered with gratitude, on several occasions, his kindness in coming to see her. She had also wondered two or three times if he was the man she vaguely remembered from her childhood; she certainly did not recognise him when they met. But she had other and more pressing things to do at present. She became very depressed at times when she dwelt upon the future, wondering how she would cope when the children grew older and, worrying, too, where they would live when Farmer Passmore needed his cottage for another workman.

She was glad when the lighter evenings came. Since Harry's death the dark evenings had seemed to be endless and she was getting short of firewood after the long cold winter.

But gradually she began to come to terms with her situation and, with the help of her cousin David and Farmer Passmore, she was able to overcome many of her difficulties. Her one great problem was loneliness and, even though her husband had not been much of a conversationalist, at least he had been there when she wished to discuss a problem.

7

It was a great relief to Jane the day Mrs Passmore came down to her cottage to tell her that she could start work at the farmhouse on the following Monday morning. She had already worked out what she would do about the children in her absence. She would take the baby with her and the elder girl, who was ten years old, would look after the two younger boys. Her daughter was a mature and sensible child and Jane felt, after talking to her, that she was capable of coping with them. But it was with some trepidation that Jane set off that Monday morning, pushing the baby in a box on wheels up the rough path to the farm. She knew that it would only be for four hours, but she had never left her children before. The risk of fire was what she feared most, but she had placed a heavy guard, which Harry had made some years previously, in front of the fire-place in order to keep the children away. She reasoned that warmer weather would soon arrive when they could play outside.

Jane enjoyed her work with Mrs Passmore; she felt so uplifted to have someone to talk with and, after her tiny cottage, the farmhouse seemed like a palace. Her mistress soon discovered Jane's ability to cook, so that became her main work.

Jane became increasingly worried about her cousin David's mental state since her husband's death. There were days when he seemed so withdrawn as not to be aware of the presence of those around him whilst, at other times, he became so aggressive that his aged mother, with whom he lived, was frightened that he might hurt someone. After work one afternoon Jane went to see her aunt to talk to her of her concern for David. The women discussed his condition at length and neither of them could understand why Harry's death had affected him so badly. The two men had never been especially close — they occasionally went to the Bear for a drink together on a Saturday evening and that, as far as the women knew, was the limit of their association.

David had refused help from anyone and this troubled his mother. She had a secret fear that her son might do as his father had done and commit suicide. She felt so helpless; if only he would talk to her. The fact that Jane felt as she did and thought it necessary to come and talk to her about it, gave her confidence to put her thoughts into action. When he came home from work one evening she took the opportunity to talk to him while he was having his meal.

'David', she said with a quiver in her voice, 'I'm very worried about you, you seem so depressed'. There was no reply. 'Don't you think it would be a good idea for you to talk to someone outside the family?' she went on. 'Why not go to the Vicar and have a chat with him?'

David's eyes glanced quickly up from his plate and down again as if surprised at his mother's suggestion. Again there was no answer, but she noticed that he stopped eating for a moment and seemed to be thinking more deeply.

'Please, David, for my sake', pleaded his mother. Then he looked up and met her tearful eyes.

'I'll think about it mother', he said, and left the house, leaving her a little more hopeful that he would co-operate.

Without telling anyone of his intentions, David set off one evening from his home in the little hamlet of Stoke, to go to the village of Hartland, about $1\frac{1}{2}$ miles away, stopping at the Bear Inn for a drink to boost his courage. As he walked up through the square in the village, past the old market cross and the remains of the market hall which had been built as long ago as 1612, to the Vicarage at the top side, he had a terrible urge to drop the whole idea and go home, but he managed to pull himself together and knocked on the door. It was opened by the maid who knew David.

'Good evening Mr Kellaway,' she said cheerfully, 'do you want to see the Vicar? I'm afraid he's having his evening meal.'

This was just the excuse for which David had hoped and he turned as if to walk away. At that moment the Revd William Chanter appeared.

'Does someone wish to see me, Mary?' he asked.

'Yes sir,' she replied, 'it's Mr Kellaway.'

David had already turned and was standing in the doorway. 'Please come in Mr Kellaway,' said the Vicar cheerfully as he ushered him into his study. 'Would you like to sit down there,' he continued, pointing to a chair beside a blazing log fire, while he seated himself on another chair on the opposite side.

David had not been a church-goer since his teenage years, but he knew his vicar and had spoken to him often when he had visited his mother. He had gone to the Vicarage in a very depressed state, but the Revd Chanter's warm welcome made him feel a little better, so he began to wonder whether or not he had made a mistake in bothering him. But he knew that he just had to share his thoughts and feelings of guilt with someone in complete confidence.

The priest could see that David had a problem on his mind, but wisely did not push him to talk about it. He enquired about his work and his mother's health — so allowing him time to give his reason for his visit. Then, without warning, David broke down and the events of that terrible night when his friend had died came pouring out between uncontrollable spasms, much of it in barely distinguishable phrases, in the form of a confession.

The vicar had been in that parish for 57 years and he had often heard rumours of the work of wreckers, but like many other people in that area had not believed them to be true. Now he was faced with the reality of the problem, and the horror of it shook him badly. He pulled himself together and turned to David, who by this time was getting control of his emotions but still very shaken. Now it was that the terrible fear of the consequences of what he had told the priest swept over him like an icy wind. Would he respect his confidence? Was his sin so terrible that he would have to take some action? He, himself, knew that he would never again take part in such an expedition but what of the others? He had not revealed their names and had no intention of doing so, but would the vicar be satisfied with his decision?

As if in answer to his questioning thoughts the vicar looked up from the fire into which he had been gazing deep in thought and, with sadness in his eyes, looked straight at David.

'Mr Kellaway,' he began in quiet but very firm tones, 'I am deeply grieved at what you have told me; it seems too horrible to be true'. He paused a moment as if too shocked to go on. Then, bracing his shoulders, he said 'I don't think I have ever heard a confession of such a serious nature in the whole of my long ministry in the Church, but I believe you are genuinely repentant of what you have done and I am thankful for that. I have not asked you the names of those who were with you that night and I have no intention of doing so. I can only hope and pray that they will be as sorry for their wrongdoing as you are'.

'Thank you sir,' David replied in a voice almost choked with emotion, 'You've got my word, I shall never do such a thing again, and I promise to help others to do what I am doing tonight'.

The priest went on to counsel David on

the spiritual aspects of his life and then gave him absolution and dismissed him with a prayer of blessing. David returned to his home much relieved that he had done what he knew he had to do. His mother immediately noticed a change in him but did not know where he had been, there was a look of peace in his face she had not seen before. Jane, too, when next she met him, realised how much more relaxed he looked and was thankful for it. She remembered so vividly that stormy night when he had come to her house bringing the news of Harry's tragic death — the look on his face had haunted her ever since but now he looked so different.

David decided never to mention the details of the January night to any of the three men who were with him. He knew that Jim Foster regretted being involved: he, like himself, was an older man and had never been very enthusiastic. It was the two younger men about whom he was most concerned. Had they been sufficiently touched by the tragedy that they would never take part in such a thing again, or would they talk, when they were in the company of their friends at the Bear, especially when they had had a little too much to drink? It was a chance he felt he would have to take.

8

Jane gradually settled down to the routine of her work at the farm but she was always glad when it was time to go home to see that all was well with the children. She found great difficulty in making the little money she received for her work meet her needs — consequently it was she who went short of food because, being the good mother she was, the children's needs came first. She was so very thankful to Mrs Passmore for giving her little bits and pieces of food from time to time which helped enormously.

The one great need for which Jane craved was companionship. This was lessened somewhat now that it was high summer and also that she had Mrs Passmore in whom she could confide but she dreaded the coming of the dark winter nights. Equally she worried that all too soon Farmer Passmore would tell her that he needed her cottage for a workman, even though she was sure he would help her in finding another. She dreaded the thought of having to leave her little home: even though she had had such unhappiness there by the death of her babies and then of her husband

and also the difficulties of providing the necessities of life for her family. But all these problems seemed to be outweighed by the sheer joy that was hers in living in such a peaceful spot, isolated though it was.

Jane had been brought up in just such a cottage as the one in which she now lived and amidst similar surroundings. She always disliked the idea of living in the village, but she was afraid she would have little choice when the time came. Houses were difficult to find with a rent she could afford to pay. She feared that her only chance would be to rent an alms house — a very poor type of dwelling administered by the local Poor Law Trust for aged people in need and others in her circumstances. She knew those houses in the village and hated the thought that she might have to live in one of them.

But Jane need not have worried. Farmer Passmore was a friend of Frank Hockin at the Quay. In conversation over a drink one evening Frank was talking about all that had been happening there since they last met.

'By the way,' he said, 'did you know that Tom Colwill is leaving us to live with his daughter in the village?'

Farmer Passmore looked up intently. 'No,' he said, 'I hadn't heard, but I'm not surprised, he must be getting on in years'.

'He certainly is,' replied Frank, 'we shall miss him very much. He has lived here all his life, I believe, and worked most of that time at the lime kilns'.

There was silence for a few moments then Farmer Passmore said, 'What do you intend to do with your cottage, Frank?'

'I haven't really thought much about it yet,' he answered.

'An idea has come to me,' went on Farmer Passmore. 'You know Jane Hickman, she does 4 hours or so a day helping my wife in the house and I need her cottage for another man'.

Already he could see that Frank was turning something over in his mind by the look in his eyes.

'I see what you're getting at,' he said, 'you would like me to let her have my cottage. The truth is,' he went on, 'my wife has been complaining lately about the amount of work she has to do here and it occurred to me while you were speaking that Jane might be the answer to our problem'.

'That would be fine, Frank,' said Farmer Passmore. 'I'll have a word with her tomorrow and bring her down to talk to your wife'.

Jane was very excited when Mrs Passmore told her of the plan when she went to work the next morning. She was thrilled at the thought of living by the sea and eagerly agreed to the suggested meeting. The following day Farmer Passmore took her to meet the Hockins. Mrs Hockin had seen Jane on two or three occasions and had been impressed by her open, kindly face, which now bore the scars of bereavement and loneliness. Jane was delighted with the outcome of the meeting when arrangements were made for her and the children to move into their new home at the end of September. Michaelmas Day was traditionally the day when farmers and farm workers changed farms and places of work.

During the three weeks before moving house Jane often found herself going back in her mind over the years she had lived in that cottage. She felt that not only would she be leaving the house she loved but, in some strange way, she would be leaving the man she loved and whom she often felt to be very close to her. She knew that the move would be good for the whole family and she must not be sentimental about it. The children were already quite excited about going to live at the Quay and all that went on there.

Jane knew that it would not be a difficult task to transport her few possessions to her new home. Moving day dawned bright and clear — a perfect autumn morning. Quite early Farmer Passmore's men arrived with a horse and wagon to collect Jane's furniture and her family. As they slowly left the cottage and were about to turn the corner by the well, Jane turned to take a last lingering look at the house that had meant so much to her, despite the many hardships she had endured there in the eleven years it had been her home. As she passed the well an unexpected thought came to her mind: she remembered it was there that she had met George Arnold when he so kindly came to console her over Harry's death. A feeling of embarrassment crept over her — she had not thought of him for a long time. She just wondered where he was and then went on to concern herself with looking after the small children as the wagon trundled down the lane through the woods to their new home.

Jane had not seen the cottage in which she was to live until she arrived with her family and furniture. It was very like her old home, which pleased her so much — but it had a tiny cottage on either side, with a wall in front which separated her flower garden from the low cliff edge. The thought at once crossed her mind that the children might be at risk, but then realised that they would soon get used to their surroundings; in any case, she would be only a few yards away from them while she worked at the hotel.

The family soon settled into their new home. It seemed strange at first to have neighbours living on either side, but a comfort to know there was someone so near. Jane was thinking ahead to the long winter nights and knew that her loneliness then would not be so intense. She was given a warm welcome next morning when she went to her work by Mrs Hockin, who had not long before started to use her home as a hotel. Jane found her work to be very different from that in Mrs Passmore's farmhouse, but much more interesting. Although the hotel was small there were people coming and going at all times. Small ships came into the harbour, bringing coal and fertilizers for local farmers and rock lime which was burnt in a kiln beside the harbour. During the summer months yachts anchored there, including those of the local squire who lived at the Abbey and sailed to and from the Mediterranean sea.

With the winter months ahead Jane felt she would have time to get used to her work before the busy summer season. There was one thing that troubled her — it was the fact that people would often be drinking in the bar until late at night. This brought back memories of the worst side of Harry's life, when he often returned from the Bear Inn on a Saturday night the worse for drink, which was something she wished to forget. But there was so much of the other side of his life — the memory of which she cherished and felt sure that she would come to terms with it all before too long.

So the months slipped quickly by and Christmas was upon them. Jane felt that this was bound to be a time for memories of years now past, when the whole family were together in their isolated little cottage. She was determined that it should be a time of joy and thanksgiving, rather than a morbid sentimentalism, especially for the sake of the children who talked less of their dad as the months passed. The Hockins were so very kind to the family at Christmas and the children enjoyed the most wonderful time they had ever known. But soon the January gales came sweeping in from the ocean, bringing back memories as the anniversary of Harry's death approached. Jane felt strangely in control of the situation and determined not to show any sadness in front of the children.

Jane had not seen her cousin David since she moved to her new home but, on the anniversary, she was sitting with her thoughts alone by the fire after putting the children to bed, when there was a tap at the door. She got up to open it with much more confidence than in former days and there stood David. She was so pleased and surprised to see him that she threw her arms around his neck, much to his embarrassment.

'Oh David,' she said excitedly, ' 'tis lovely to see you. Come on in'. She placed a chair for him by the fire and seated herself opposite him. She noticed at once how much more calm and relaxed he had become since she last saw him.

'I felt I just had to come and see you this evening, Jane,' he said quietly with a tinge of sadness in his voice.

She knew what he meant and there was a long silence, each not knowing quite what to say next. Jane deliberately turned their thoughts away from what she knew was on both their minds.

'How's your mother David?' she asked, with the obvious effects of those thoughts still plain in her voice.

David quietly replied, 'She's very well, thanks Jane, and would like to see you.' Unlike the David of old he went on, 'She knows it won't be 'til the weather improves and you can get up the cliff road. She would like to know how the children are keeping'.

'They're very well and enjoying their new

home,' Jane replied. 'Tell your mother I'll see her as soon as I can.'

They went on to talk about mutual friends but avoided any mention of Harry's death. As he rose to leave after having had a cup of tea, David said, 'I'm delighted you are so happy and comfortable here, Jane. May God bless you.' Jane was so taken aback at what he said that she could only reply in muffled tones 'Thanks David, see you again soon'.

His words were to remain with her for a long time — they were so unlike the language of the David she had known in the past. Even as he spoke them she had seen a light in his eyes which was much more than a reflection from the little oil lamp she held in her hand as she opened the door for him to leave.

9

It seemed such a short time before the first signs of spring began to show in Jane's little garden in front of her cottage and the snowdrops and crocuses and a little later the daffodils began to push their heads through the soil. New life was bursting out all around and Jane, too, felt a stirring within her that was almost akin to a sexual desire. She felt uneasy about this and wondered why it should be; then she remembered that she had experienced such feelings many times in her teenage years while working at the big house. Since Harry's death she had had no thoughts for other men, but lately she had found herself looking admiringly or otherwise at young men who came into the hotel. At first she felt terribly guilty, but after a while she was able to control her feelings and live a normal life.

Jane's peace of mind was not to last for long. Since starting work at the hotel she had begun to take more interest in her appearance. Her hair was now always tidy, her clothes and her person much cleaner than in the old days before her husband's death.

She was a very attractive young woman — a fact that was not lost on John Cann who lived in Hartland village some three miles away and who came to the hotel twice each week delivering bread and other provisions, with a horse and a covered van.

John was several years younger than Jane and he knew of her circumstances. She had noticed him looking at her from time to time as she carried away the goods he had brought into the storeroom. She had not felt unduly disturbed by his attentions until one day he accidentally touched her while passing loaves of bread from the van. Jane blushed deeply and felt sure the young man could detect her feelings of excitement. She quickly turned away with the bread in her hands and made an excuse to do something else until he had gone.

From the first day he met Jane, John had longed to be able to talk to her at length instead of the few words they exchanged each time he came to the hotel, but found it hard to bring himself to put the question. He knew that if she agreed to see him, it would have to be in her home because she could not leave the children to meet him anywhere else. Even then, it would be after they had gone to bed. As he drove back to the village that day John struggled within himself as to how he could muster the courage to do what he longed to do more than anything else.

Jane's attraction to the young man seemed to take on a strange twist and held her back from thinking about him. It was a feeling that she was being disloyal. But to whom? She had carefully thought about her future as far as other men were concerned and wondered if she would be disloyal to Harry if she met someone whom she could love and trust. She was sure that the children's security, and her own, would be his desire for them.

For several weeks Jane avoided being alone with John, until one day Mrs Hockin asked her to tell him to put the goods in another part of the house. Alterations were being made which involved a new area for the things to be stored. When they were alone in the storeroom John felt an urge to take advantage of that opportunity to ask Jane if he could come to her house after the children had gone to bed, to talk with her. He almost missed the chance because of his shyness but just as they were coming out of the room he blurted out, 'Oh Jane, would you mind if I came and had a chat with you one evening?' There was no reply as she closed the door behind her and began to walk back to the kitchen with John wondering if he had offended her. But then she allowed herself to look up into his face as he walked beside her. He looked so young and, she imagined, so inexperienced in the responsibilities of life — surely there could be no harm in allowing him to come to her home for a few minutes. Just before they were about to go their separate ways, it was as if she heard herself saying, 'Yes, John, I would like you to come.' John was so embarrassed that he quite forgot to ask her which evening it should be. It was not until he was about to drive away that he remembered and a date was arranged; and he went off a very happy young man.

As the time for John's visit approached Jane found herself becoming a little disturbed yet, at the same time, there was an excitement she had not known before — even when she first met Harry. As soon as she got home from work at the hotel that evening she began to busy herself about the house — cleaning and tidying after the children had gone to bed. Then she spent a little time on her own person, brushing her hair and making herself as attractive as possible and, at the same time, creating a self-confidence to face what she felt would be an emotional evening.

It had not been her habit to talk to the children about her deeper feelings when their father died — even less so about her thoughts on this particular evening. She had been brought up to believe that it was wrong to share such thoughts with children, but her daughter was now eleven years old and just had to be told that a friend was coming to see her mum. The child accepted this without question, having been subjected to her father's very strict discipline all her life — discipline which Jane had sometimes felt to be excessive.

At last the time for John's arrival drew near. Jane could not relax but continued to fuss around the room, moving this and altering that. Then there came a tap on the door, so light as to be almost unnoticeable. At last the moment to which Jane had looked forward, but which she now almost dreaded, had arrived. What should she say to him? There was no time to think about that anymore — the door was open and there she was — face to face with the young man who had been so much in her thoughts. It was with a voice that was almost a whisper that she said, 'Come in, John. Sit in that chair', and she pointed to a rather ragged old armchair that had seen better days.

John seemed more embarrassed than Jane as they sat on opposite sides of the fireplace. He could not bring himself to look at her, but kept his eyes on the flickering flame which licked around the logs of wood and from which blue smoke lazily curled up the open chimney. It was Jane who ended the uncomfortable silence: 'Would you like a cup of tea John?' she asked. This was just the break he needed.

'Oh yes please, Jane,' he replied with enthusiasm.

The conversation for the remainder of the evening was much more relaxed. They talked about the children and Jane's work at the hotel, and about each other's families. All too soon for John it was time for him to begin his three mile walk back to his home in the village. Both young people were feeling much happier as they stood in the doorway together for a moment, when John suddenly said, 'Goodnight Jane, thanks for having me,' and set off up the steep hill to the cliff top. It was a lovely autumn night and the murmur of the waves gently breaking upon the rocks below seemed to fit his feeling of peace and contentment with all that had taken place that evening. Just one thing troubled him: he regretted having been so shy when in Jane's company and wished he could have told her of his feelings for her. He determined to be more of a man when next he went to see her.

Then it was he remembered that he had

forgotten to arrange a date for their next meeting, but felt more at ease when he realised he would see her again in two days time when he made his usual delivery of bread. He was now passing the 15th century parish church with its 144 feet high tower which seemed to reach up through the autumn mists to the stars beyond his view. The whole building seemed to John to stand for something strong and lasting, which gave him a feeling of security and self-confidence for the future. So he squared his shoulders and strode on towards his home, his heavy nailed boots clattering on the rough stoney road.

John continued to meet Jane at her home quite frequently during the autumn months of that year. For a while she found comfort in his company, especially when the first storms began to sweep in from the sea and caused the wind to rear around her little cottage which had no protection from the gales. She sometimes longed for her old home — isolated as it was — and the shelter of the deep wooded valley. But Jane was thankful that she was so near to friends in case of need.

Jane had noticed a change coming over her new friend during his visits, which disturbed her a little. He was losing some of his shyness which she felt was good, but he often showed a side of his nature which tended to upset her. She had been used to Harry's almost overpowering sexual advances which he sometimes displayed, but had not expected it from a young man like John who had been so reserved. But there was something that troubled her more than his occasional outbursts: this was the fact that she herself often felt an urge to co-operate, and although she resisted, she sometimes did so with great difficulty. These episodes generally ended with Jane taking a tough line and telling John that if he wished to continue visiting her he must behave properly. On several occasions she felt very relieved when the weather was so bad that he was unable to come to her; yet at the same time, she secretly found pleasure in his company.

10

Almost two years had passed since the night that Harry Hickman died. The two youngest members of the group which accompanied him on that fateful expedition, Archie Martin and Bill Brown, were at the Bear one evening when John Cann walked in. He had been on his way to see Jane, when a terrible storm accompanied by heavy rain had swept in with the tide, causing him to cancel his visit. So he decided that having walked two miles of the journey he would go into the Bear for a drink before returning home.

John did not care much for alcohol and never felt at ease in a pub, so he was delighted when he found Archie and Bill, who lived near to him in the village, sitting in front of a lovely fire; here, too, he was able to dry his wet clothes. He had never before spent much time in the company of these two young men — they being a little older than he and much more experienced in the seamy side of life as it existed at that time in Hartland. They both worked as labourers on the Abbey estate.

The two friends made John very welcome

and bought him a pint of cider. The conversation that followed was of a general nature: mainly about the storm they could hear raging outside and its effect upon the shipping in the area. They reckoned that it would have caught most vessels unprepared by its sudden appearance and severity. John, of course, knew nothing of their involvement in Jane's husband's death — in fact, they themselves had spoken very little about it, even to one another, since that night when they had been so shocked. But they were very insensitive young men and time was already healing some of those memories.

As the three men sat staring into the fire Archie looked up and caught Bill's eye. 'I say Bill,' he said, excitedly, 'How about going down to the beach presently, after the tide has turned, to see if there is anything worth picking up?'

Bill agreed at once and went on, 'What about you, John, would you like to come?'

John hesitated. 'No thanks,' he replied, 'I don't think I will. You see, I have to start work at 5 o'clock in the morning'.

'We shan't stay more than an hour,' Archie went on.

'Oh well, in that case, I think I will come with you,' John answered almost reluctantly. He became more and more interested as his friends talked about what they might find and after about two hours the gale abated somewhat, so the three men set off for the cliffs. Between breaks in the cloud the full moon lighted their way down the treacherous path to the beach below, where the exceptionally high tide had already begun to ebb. They scrambled along over the pebbles for some time, all the while keeping a watch seaward through the foaming waters for any ship that might have hit the rocks.

It was John who made the gruesome discovery when, as the moon came out from behind a cloud, he saw at his feet the body of a man, still fully clothed and which had obviously not been in the water for a long period. John had not come face to face with death before and he was badly shaken. The other two men who had more experience took over the situation and, after examining the body, decided that the man was dead. After consulting together they agreed that one of them had to go either to the hotel or to Passmore's farm to find something with which to carry the body from the beach.

So it was Bill who set off for the hotel while Archie and John prepared for what they knew would be a long wait for his return. As the minutes passed John became more and more restless and disturbed — all thoughts of looking for anything on the beach had been dashed by the discovery of the body. John wished he had not come: if he was late for work in the morning he might lose his job at the bakery.

'I shall have to go home,' he shouted close to Archie's ear because of the noise of the gale that continued to blow. He was still shocked at what he had discovered and wanted to get away from it all. Archie did not answer, but was looking further along the beach beyond some high rocks. At that moment, there was another break in the clouds and the moon lit up the whole scene as bright as day.

'Can you see something sticking up beyond those rocks over there John?' he shouted, pointing in the direction of a high ridge.

John looked a little more intently. 'Yes Archie,' he replied ,'It looks like the mast of a ship'.

That was enough to set Archie bounding along the beach and scrambling up the slippery slope of the rocks with John close behind. On reaching the top they clearly saw the outline of a vessel, which appeared to be completely out of the water. Archie became very excited: to find a ship in this way was beyond his wildest dreams. All kinds of thoughts raced through his mind as he slid down the other side. It was almost certain, he felt, that the dead man had been a member of the crew of this ship. But what was it carrying and would there be anyone on board?

When they reached the vessel they found her to be high and dry, leaning against the foot of the towering cliff. They stood for a moment, gazing up at her and Archie noticed that her name was 'Arria' which did not seem very English to him. They decided to try to attract the attention of anyone who might be on board by shouting together, but their voices were as nothing compared with the roar of the wind and the pounding of the waves.

Archie then started to scramble up the boarding rope, while John — too scared to follow him — watched in fear. Archie reached the desk just for'ard of the bridge on which he found a man standing motionless. He seemed to be holding on to the rail with one hand, as if to support himself in the gale, whilst the other hand was in his pocket. Archie was just about to speak when suddenly the man took his hand out of his pocket and was holding what appeared to be a revolver on which the moonlight glinted. Almost immediately the sound of a shot rang out above the noise of the storm, followed quickly by another. Archie felt nothing, so assumed he was unhurt and without stopping to ask questions he dived over the side, almost missing the rope in his hurry to escape from what he felt would be certain death. He hid among the rocks for a while to recover his breath and then quietly made his way back to where he expected to find Bill but there was no sign of John.

Archie had never been so frightened in his life. Like John, he wished he had not come there that night. But why, he wondered, had the skipper of that vessel — he assumed it was the skipper — been prepared to take such drastic action. Had he been warned of what might happen to him and his ship if ever he was wrecked on that coast? By the time Archie reached the position of the body Bill had returned with a makeshift stretcher, but there was still no sign of John. So the two men began the laborious trek over the pebbles and rocks carrying the dead man to the hotel where the Hockins were once again called into action. It was not until they were making their way home that Archie could bring himself to tell Bill all that had happened during his absence. Bill, like his friend, was shocked and spoke very little all the way to the village.

John had watched Archie scramble over the deck rail and disappear from his sight. Then he heard the first shot which he thought was the sound of wreckage crashing on to the rocks. But when the second shot rang out he knew what it was and just turned and ran with no thought for Archie's safety. On and on he struggled, along the beach and up the rough cliff path, his heart pounding and his lungs gasping. He had never before been in such a frightening experience; but now he just had to stop and rest and give himself time to think what to do next. His mind was in a whirl — he could not work things out clearly. Above all else he felt a terrible sense of guilt. First that he had allowed himself to become involved that evening — it was not his way of life. But the second thought hurt him even more — he had deserted his friend in his time of need. He sought to excuse himself by arguing that he was in no fit state to help at the time, in any case, if Archie was dead there was no point in going back — perhaps to get shot himself. So he set off for home again — a very weary and downcast young man, to arrive there just two hours before it was time to start work.

John had no appetite for breakfast that morning and when he looked at himself in the mirror he was shocked to see how haggard and drawn he had become. It was his day to deliver bread at Jane's place of work and as he drove the horse and van towards the hotel he wondered how she would react when she saw his condition. He secretly hoped that they would not meet that day, even though he longed for her comforting words. But he had another problem. Should he tell Jane what had happened that night? After thinking about it for a while he decided that he must take her into his confidence because she would be sure to hear about it at the hotel.

When John arrived that afternoon Jane was not to be seen. Should he look for her or just unload and go straight back to the village? He decided on the latter course and sped up the cliff road as fast as the horse could pull the van. But he had not gone far when he met the local policeman on his bicycle who stopped to ask him questions about the body found on the beach the previous evening. It was obvious to John that the officer knew who was present when it was discovered, so he assumed that Archie or Bill had been interviewed by him.

John had begun to shake when first stopped by the policeman, but surprised himself at the speed with which he was able to relax and give a clear account of what happened that night. He took care, however, not to mention anything about finding the vessel and the shots being fired and hoped that his friends had not done so either. The officer seemed satisfied with the replies he had received and went on his way to the hotel.

John felt that he just had to see his friends that evening to hear what had passed between them and the police officer. He was afraid, too, that they might accuse him of deserting them but when they eventually met near his home they seemed quite friendly towards him and he was pleased to know that Archie was uninjured. In relating his experiences while on the deck of that ship Archie admitted that he had never been so scared in all his life. It was later revealed at the inquest on the drowned man, by the captain, that he knew of several skippers who had armed themselves as he had done, to protect themselves and their ships from wreckers on that coast, if ever they were unfortunate enough to be driven ashore.

When Jane heard that John had been involved in the discovery of the body on the beach she was disturbed and very surprised that he had allowed himself to be drawn into the company of such men as Bill Brown and Archie Martin, who, she knew, to be rather rough characters. She wished she could talk to John and get his version of the affair.

She had not long to wait. Late in the evening of the day after John had met the policeman, a very light tap on her door was enough to tell her that her hopes were realised. On the way to the door she felt a flush of excitement filling her whole being; she felt again like a teenage girl meeting her boyfriend as she tidied her hair with her hands before lifting the latch.

Jane had quite a shock when she opened the door and saw John looking so pale after his ordeal two nights previously. 'Oh John,' she blurted out, 'whatever has happened? you look so ill', all the while longing to hold him in her arms.

John did not reply until he was seated opposite her in front of the fire. Then he sheepishly started to tell her what happened that night. 'I wish I hadn't gone, Jane,' he began, like a little boy confessing a wrong doing. 'I ought to have known that nothing good could have come out of that company'.

After he had described finding the body — details of which he spared Jane — he went on to tell her how they had discovered the ship and all that followed. At this stage he seemed to be reliving that nightmare and, as all the fears came rushing back, his face became deathly pale and his body shook. 'Why was I such a fool, Jane, why was I such a fool?' was all he could say.

Jane could restrain herself no longer. 'Dear John,' she murmured, taking his hands in hers as she knelt by his chair, 'all that is passed; it has gone and you are safe with me'.

She was very surprised when she realised what she was saying but all her motherly instincts were, at that moment, concentrated on John and his need. She felt no regret at what she had said.

'Thanks Jane,' said John. 'I wish I could have come to you that night but I've learned my lesson never to go with those chaps again'.

He looked such a pathetic figure as he responded to Jane's words of comfort. He rose from his chair and put an arm around her shoulder and held her close but without the aggression he had shown on previous occasions. As he felt the warmth of her body so close to his own, a body that had become more beautiful and a little more buxom since her living conditions had improved, he whispered, 'You are wonderful, Jane. I love you so much'.

Jane had begun by acting like a mother rather than a girlfriend and had intended to keep it that way but John's gentle approach, the nearness of his body and his strong arms around her brought out all the pent-up sexual desires that she had suppressed for so long. She was only able to murmur, 'I love you too, John,' before their lips met in a final embrace.

11

Some two years after returning to Wales and resuming his work aboard ship, George Arnold was promoted by his company and given command of a small coaster carrying coal out of Barry, as he had done while acting as first mate on other boats. His thoughts often turned to Jane and her little cottage, as he travelled from port to port. At first he did his best to dismiss such thoughts as being rather silly for a man of his age but, as time passed, he had to admit that he was attracted to her although he could not come to the point of making contact with her.

These feelings had been especially strong in George when, on two or three occasions, he had brought his ship into the port of Bideford with a cargo of coal. He realised at such times that he was only just 14 miles from Jane and felt especially close to her.

On one such trip, when his ship was tied up at Bideford quay and the cargo was being discharged, George decided to take a walk along the river bank to get some exercise. Next but one to his ship he passed another vessel from which agricultural fertiliser was being unloaded into farm wagons, each drawn by two horses. His attention was fixed on a man who was arranging the two hundredweight bags of manure in his wagon as they were dropped there by a crane, while a dozen or more others waited their turn to load.

The man seemed vaguely familiar to George although he could not give him a name or even say where he had seen him before. As he watched the man at work it felt as if a sort of depression was creeping over him; he suddenly felt unhappy, but could give no reason for it. It was a lovely day and everything was going well for him. Why this sudden feeling of sadness? George went to take a closer look at the man; then, like a flash, something clicked in his mind. Of course — it was the man who had been on the beach the night his captain was drowned and he himself had almost lost his life — the man who was with him at the inquest when they had to identify the two bodies.

All the memories of that terrible night swept over George in that moment like a wave but then, just as quickly, everything changed. Another memory seemed to smother the unhappiness and stand out bright and clear. It was that of the young widow whose image so often filled his thoughts and to whom he had become so attracted. He was overjoyed and felt that he must speak to the man.

That man was David Kellaway, Jane's cousin, who at that time was head horseman on the Abbey estate. George walked over to the wagon and, leaning on the rail, he looked up at David. 'Excuse me,' he said, 'I think I have seen you before, but can't remember your name'.

David looked down from the top of his load which was now almost complete. For a moment he hesitated then, in a flash, he realised who it was who spoke to him even though he could not remember his name, either. It was as if, in that moment, all the associations he had had with that man were pictured before his eyes and a sadness filled his heart.

'Hullo,' he said, as cheerfully as he could, 'yes, we have met, but I'm afraid I've forgotten your name, too. I'm David Kellaway and we last met at the inquest at Hartland Quay'.

David had no wish to talk about their first meeting on the beach. 'Fancy meeting you here,' he said. 'Are you on one of the boats?'

George was watching David closely as he was speaking and realised there was something different about the man since he last saw him. He looked so calm and relaxed now — there was a wonderful peace in his eyes, whereas just two years previously he looked to be on the verge of a nervous breakdown.

'Yes,' replied George. 'There she is, the 'Cwmbrae' next to the bridge', pointing towards the end of the line of ships being discharged.

He was rather hesitant to ask David about Jane directly. 'How are the Hockins at the Quay?' he continued, remembering their kindness to him during his stay at the hotel.

'They are very well,' said David. 'They have had a busy summer with several yachts coming in, as well as the normal shipping. But they have help in the hotel now — my cousin Jane, whom I believe you met, lives in one of the cottages there and works for Mrs Hockin'.

This was just what George had hoped to hear. 'Is your cousin well and happier now?' he queried. 'Oh yes,' answered David. 'She is very well and loves her new home. The children are happy too and like living by the sea'.

David began to prepare for his journey. 'I'm afraid I must be on my way,' he said.

'It gets dark much earlier now and I have a long way to go'. Picking up the reins and preparing to clambour on to the front of the wagon he held out his hand to George. 'Cheerio then,' he said. 'It's been good to see you again under different circumstances. I hope all goes well for you'.

George shook hands with David and wished him well too, with the hope that they would meet again. So David set off with his team up the steep hill out of the town and headed for home. That brief contact had filled George's heart with joy. He was so thankful that Jane was happier and he wondered if she ever thought of him. He determined to see her again if it was at all possible.

12

Life for David Kellaway had changed completely since his first visit to the Vicar. It was as if a light had come into his life — a desire to know more of the deeper things of life. The Revd William Chanter had kept in regular contact with him ever since that night when David had been so disturbed and they had had many long talks.

David had been brought up to attend church as a boy but, like many others, he went less and less during his teenage years. Recently he had become a bellringer and was taking an increasing interest in all that went on in connection with church life. The most encouraging thing for the Vicar when they talked together was David's gradual spiritual development. He had quite a bright mind and felt that he would like to learn to read and write. He put the idea to Mr Chanter who at once arranged for him to attend evening classes with a Mr Heard who ran a Dame School in the village. He made wonderful progress and was soon able to read simple passages from his bible which the Vicar had given him.

There was much controversy at that time between members of the Anglican Church and some non-conformist groups in the parish, which troubled a lot of people. David was anxious to learn all he could about the Christian religion, but as yet he had only been in contact with the Anglican tradition. He had not long to wait to hear about another aspect of the Faith.

He and some friends, including Bill and Archie, were in the King's Arms pub one evening, having a quiet drink, when a stranger walked into the bar asking for food. He said that he had discovered the love of Christ and felt that he ought to tell his fellow men the story of Christ's love for them and persuade them, if possible, to come to Him as their Saviour. He said he felt too timid to speak in public before his own neighbours yet, longing to say something for Christ, he thought it would be best to go to some place where he was unknown. So he had walked all the way from Callington in Cornwall to Hartland where no-one knew him and he knew no-one, except one friend.

After he finished his refreshments he said to the landlord, 'Did you ever see a Methodist preacher?'

'No Sir,' he said. 'I've heard of them but never seen one'.

'Well, then, I am one and I should like to preach here in your parlour if you will allow me'.

'Oh, but you see, Sir, the parson lives just up at the top of the Square!' replied the rather frustrated hotelier.

'Never mind the parson, my good friend,' the man replied. 'I am not afraid of him. Shall I preach?'

'It'll make the room very dirty, I'm afraid Sir,' said the landlord. 'We shall have so many people here'.

'Will you agree to let me preach if I pay all the expense of cleaning?'

'I suppose I must, then, Sir'.

So it was arranged that the landlord should tell everybody who came to the pub and get them to tell others that a Methodist preacher was going to preach there the next evening but one. When the time came the place was full. The man wondered what to do about the singing, then he remembered how the landlord had mentioned the parson so he thought that if he pitched to the tune of the 'Old Hundreth' psalm they would, as church goers, be able to join in. They sang like larks.

When it came to the time for the sermon the man found it hard to keep himself from letting the people see him trembling. He said later, 'I began in the strength of the Lord and was able to tell them what God had done for my soul'. He was listened to very quietly, but before he could give out the last hymn a man cried out, 'Have you finished, Sir'.

'Yes,' replied the preacher.

'Oh,' was the response. 'It was very good, Sir. Will you please say it all over again, Sir?'

'Well my friend,' the preacher said, 'I don't know that I could say it over again exactly as before, but if you like to stay a little longer I'll try to say something more to you'.

'Do that Sir, do that,' cried many voices. 'It is very good'.

So he began again and gave another address, after which the two young men, Archie and Bill, were so deeply impressed that they came to him again the next evening seeking further instruction.

On the following Sunday morning the preacher walked out to the parish church. The Vicar had heard of what had been happening in the pub and thought it necessary to warn his flock against the man whom, he said, was a false teacher. He told his congregation that the man's doctrine was untrue. The Methodist preacher waited in the churchyard after the service and, when the Vicar came out, he asked to be allowed to speak to him. He listened carefully and the man said:

'I heard you preach this morning, Sir, with great surprise. I liked you while you read the prayers but your sermon gave me pain'.

'What do you mean, Sir?' said the Vicar with a note of anger in his voice. 'Get along about your business,' and, joining some friends, he went off, leaving the man to solve the difference between the sermon and the prayer.

Next morning the Vicar sent a footman to the King's Arms, asking for the preacher who, on hearing his name mentioned, came to the door.

'Here I am,' he said. 'What can I do for you?'

'Master wants to know by whose authority you insulted him in the churchyard yesterday?'

'Authority!' replied the preacher. 'I had no authority to insult him; I did not intend to insult him and am sorry if I seemed to do so. But I have authority for what I said'.

He then took his prayer book and tried to show the footman what he had meant when speaking to the Vicar.

'Give my respects to your master,' he said, 'and show him the places in the prayer book which I have shown you and ask him, from me, to think about them seriously'.

The footman walked off, shrugged his shoulders, and the preacher heard no more from the Vicar.

Archie and Bill became more and more interested in what they had learnt from the Methodist preacher, so along with several others they formed a group which met each Sunday in the home of an old lady called Miss Trelevan, who was a friend of the Methodist gentleman from Callington.

David Kellaway was not so impressed by what he had heard as were his two younger friends. He was unable to accept what seemed to him to be the man's unnatural enthusiasm. After giving it a great deal of thought he decided to stay with the Church and its teachings in which he had been brought up and with Mr Chanter, who had helped him so much in the past.

Since his conversation David had become a great comfort to his aged mother with whom he lived. There was a sparkle in his eyes now and a lightness in his step which made him look years younger. He loved his work, hard though it was, and he looked forward to each day with joy.

David was a simple countryman who took a keen interest in nature and the changing seasons. As he followed his team of horses in the plough the many seagulls and other birds which accompanied them held a great fascination for him. When he sat in the hedge eating his lunch each day, while the horses munched the grass contentedly, David quietly sought to relate all this and the beauty around him with what he heard in church each Sunday. Although he realised there was so much he could not understand, yet these thoughts gave him a wonderful peace of mind and a desire to share it with others less fortunate than himself.

It was almost dark one late autumn evening as David slowly plodded his way home to the stables, riding one of his team and leading the other, after a hard day's ploughing. He was thinking of his mother; how pleased she would be to see him after being alone all day. It suddenly occurred to him that he knew several elderly housebound men and women in his village who would have no-one to come home to them that evening or any other evening and who would spend the long dark hours alone. Something stirred in him and he could not get the idea out of his mind.

As he watered and fed his horses and bedded them down for the night David could think of nothing else but the joy it would bring those old people to have someone come into their homes to talk with them. Before leaving the stable he had made up his mind that he would do just that instead of spending so much time most evenings in the pubs. His mother was delighted when he told her of his plan and suggested that he should start by going to see a cousin of hers who, like herself, was confined to her home and whom she had not seen for nearly two years.

This was the beginning of a wonderfully fruitful experience for David. In giving himself in this way he came to know such a fulness of life that was beyond anything he could have imagined. Most of the people he visited lived in the Almshouses with barely enough food and heat to keep them alive — especially during the winter months. Many of them had lived in the parish all their lives and some were without relatives to visit them. It was such a comfort to those elderly people to have him spend an hour or so with them occasionally, bringing news of what was happening in the parish and sometimes helping them with their problems. He often played cards with them — and a game called Don was a great favourite.

He occasionally had difficulties when visiting. He was with a very old man one evening, talking about the past as elderly people love to do, when the man started to tell of wrecking experiences in which he had been involved as a young man. David found this conversation to be disturbing, it brought back too many unhappy memories. He gently turned the conversation to other things and the old man seemed quite happy to accept it. What they talked about mattered very little to him, as long as there was someone to share the evening with him.

When David came home from work one evening in the following Spring, he was surprised to find Jane talking with his mother.

'Hello Jane,' he said. 'Fancy seeing you here'. Then he noticed that Jane did not look her usual happy self that he had come to know since her friendship with John Cann had developed.

'Hello David,' she said in a voice that was almost choked with emotion. 'I hope you're all right'.

'Yes,' he replied. 'I'm fine, but . . .' Here his mother intervened and suggested he should sit down and let Jane tell him what she had told her.

Jane went on to say how worried she was about John's health. Ever since the night they had found the body on the beach and he had afterwards ran home in fear he had not felt at all well.

'Have you seen him lately David?' she asked. 'He looks so haggard and pale and he's losing weight, too'.

'No,' replied David, 'I haven't seen him for several weeks, but don't worry too much, Jane, he may have been over working — you know what long hours he puts in each day'.

'I don't think it is that,' said Jane. 'I wish he could get help but all he says when I mention it to him is, 'I shall be all right'. 'I wish you could have a chat with him David,' his mother said, 'and try to persuade him to see old Mrs Mumford'.

Mrs Mumford — old Mother Mumford as she was known to everyone — was an elderly lady who had been widowed many years and who had inherited the art of healing all kinds of sicknesses with herbal remedies. She also 'charmed' certain conditions with words known only to her and handed down by her mother and forebears, which was expected to bring healing. Mother Mumford was the only person to whom people in the parish could turn when they were ill. The nearest apothecary was 14 miles away and there were no doctors.

It was several days before David managed to meet up with John and he realised at once that Jane's fears were by no means unfounded. The young man looked terrible and at once the thought swept through his mind — consumption, or 'decline' as it was known locally. It was then that he remembered that John's mother and two teenage sisters had died of the same disease. David's first thoughts were for Jane, that she should have to be subjected again to a heart-breaking bereavement so soon after the first. He knew that medically speaking there was little that could be done if John had that condition, but he must see Mrs Mumford.

The two men had met in the village square, near to John's home, just as he was about to set off to walk the three miles to see Jane.

'Hullo there, young John,' David shouted from across the street. 'Haven't seen you for a long time; how are you?'

'Oh, not so bad thanks', replied John in a voice that David thought to be much less robust than once it was.

'I saw Jane the other day and she said you weren't too well'.

'Jane worries too much,' said John. 'I believe she thinks I'm still a little boy who needs mothering'.

'But she is concerned about you John,' David said very firmly, 'and you really ought to get someone to help you, for her sake as well as your own'.

'Perhaps you're right David,' said John in a voice that really was like that of a little boy. 'I don't seem to have much breath these days — even to walk out to Jane's place is a real struggle'.

'Then will you go up and see Mother Mumford?'

'Yes, all right David, I will if you think it is right'.

A sense of sadness filled David's heart as he watched the young man start his walk to meet the girl who had given him so much hope and changed his life. David noticed that his shoulders were slouched forward and he seemed to be dragging his legs as if his heavy nailed boots were holding him back. He felt that he should not be putting his body to the strain of such a long walk while in that condition and he longed to help him.

As he set off in the direction of the Almshouses the idea came to David that he should talk to the Vicar about John's problem. He remembered how, only on the previous Sunday in church, he had heard the story of the healing of the sick man who had been brought to Jesus by four friends. Could not the same be done for John, he wondered? David decided not to wait until Sunday before sharing his thoughts with Mr

Chanter, but to see him in his Vicarage the next evening.

While walking up the path to see the Vicar the memory of another such visit came to his mind — of the night he needed help so badly. He thought of the broken, depressed man who felt himself to be such a failure — an individual to whom the future looked meaningless. How different now as he knocked on the door with confidence. No turning away this time when the maid opened the door but, with a light in his eyes, he walked into the Vicar's study and shook hands with Mr Chanter.

David at once raised the question of John's illness and suggested that the Vicar might like to visit him if John so wished. This the Vicar agreed to do, adding that he would be praying for John. He thanked David for coming to talk to him and dismissed him with his blessing.

John kept his promise to David and after work one evening he shyly walked up to Mother Mumford's dilapidated old cottage where she had lived all her life. In the forefront of his mind, all the while, was the horrible memory he had tried so hard to forget for the past ten years, when his sisters had been so ill and finally died of consumption. Surely, he felt, he could not have that disease — he had been told that only women went into decline.

Before he could dwell any more on his illness he was knocking on the door of the cottage which slowly opened on its squeaking hinges to reveal a little old lady in a dazzlingly white apron. Her eyes sparkled and a lovely smile spread over her face as she welcomed John into her kitchen.

'What can I do for you, young man?' she said, her voice echoing like a peal of bells.

John was barely audible as he replied, 'I don't seem able to breathe very well and I've got an awful cough'.

Mother Mumford's expression changed as she looked more closely at him in the dim light of her tiny oil lamp.

'Sit down and tell me all about it,' she said, pointing to a settle — a high-backed wooden settle, to be found in the front of the open fire of almost every home in those days, where one could sit free from draughts that whistled in through badly fitting doors and windows. She watched him as he crossed the room and slumped rather than sat; she saw the tell-tale signs with which she had become so familiar during her long life.

The room was spotlessly clean and around the walls there was shelf upon shelf of bottles, jars and tins of every description containing decoctions she had made from many kinds of herbs, flowers and vegetables and which she used for ailments of so many kinds. There was an iron crock hanging over the fire in which another mixture bubbled and gurgled before being made ready to be put on the shelf.

'How long have you had this trouble?' she asked, seating herself on a chair opposite to John and watching his breathing closely.

'About five months, I think,' he replied. 'It seemed to start after I was very frightened one night and ran up a cliff path'. He then went on to tell the old lady of his experience the night he and his friends had found the body on the beach.

'Do you cough up blood?' she asked almost reluctantly.

'I have done two or three times,' he said, his voice trembling as with fear.

'I expect you know what is wrong with you,' she went on.

John looked up with a start — his eyes expressing his deeper feelings.

'It can't be decline, can it? I didn't think men had that'.

'I'm afraid that's what it is', she replied. 'Men do get it sometimes as well as women'. There was a sadness in her voice now — she felt so sorry for this young man just coming into manhood. 'I'll give you something to help you,' and Mother Mumford took four jars from a shelf and mixed Borage, Rosemary, Cabbage and Safflower together. This mixture was regularly used to treat consumption — in fact it was the only known remedy at that time.

John thanked the old lady and gave her four pence, which was all he had. As he rose to leave the house she laid her hands upon his chest and mumbled some words which he could not understand and wished him goodnight.

The walk home was a sad one for John. Although he had felt for some time that he might be going into decline he kept putting the thought away and hoping he was wrong. Mother Mumford's diagnosis had been a bitter blow to him and he longed to be able to talk to Jane about the whole thing. By the time he reached home he was too shattered to undertake the long walk to see her that night. He had to be content to share the bad news with his father with whom he lived.

John and his father had never been very close, even though they had been left together when his mother died when he was eight years old — and later his two sisters had also died. Mr Cann had brought up his son under difficult circumstances and without help. He had become a very morose and unhappy man and when John told him what Mother Mumford had said it was more than he could take and he broke down completely, threatening to take his life. All this frightened John — he had never seen his father in such a state. Then he had the idea to ask David to come and talk to him — they having been lifelong friends.

John was determined to see Jane the following evening and, when he at last arrived at her home, he was completely exhausted. It gave her quite a shock to see how ill he looked. After telling her about his visit to Mrs Mumford he paused as if not knowing what to say; then he almost burst into tears: 'Oh Jane, do you think I shall get well again?'

Jane was not prepared for such a question and could only put an arm around his shoulder and whisper, 'You will take what Mother Mumford has given you, won't you?' As she held him close to herself he became again as a little boy, needing so much to be comforted and she remembered so vividly her own mother's condition before she died of the same disease when Jane was 16 years old. She could see the same symptoms in John as he sprawled in a chair, completely exhausted after his long walk.

13

Several months had passed since John had seen his friends Archie and Bill, then he met them one evening in the Square on their way to the weekly meeting of the Methodist group. They had been told of John's illness but did not expect to see him looking quite so bad.

'Hello John', said Archie as cheerily as he could. 'Haven't seen you for ages'.

'No,' replied John, weakly, 'I'm still here, but only just'.

'Oh, come off it, ol' chap,' said Bill. 'Things aren't as bad as all that, are they?'

The two young men were obviously shocked to hear John talking in this way, it was so unlike him.

'Why not come with us, John,' Bill continued. 'We are going up to our little meeting; you'd enjoy an hour with us'.

John hesitated for a while. Jane had told him not to come to her in the evenings for a while, but to be content just to see her for a few minutes when he made his twice weekly delivery to the hotel.

'All right chaps,' he answered. 'I'll come

with you'. So they set off for the home of Miss Trelevan where they were warmly welcomed by the little group of people already assembled in her kitchen.

Miss Trelevan was an educated lady who had come to live in the village a few years previously, so the reading of the bible together with prayer and the singing of well-known hymns, followed by a general discussion, made up the evening's programme. Both John and Archie had been to Mr Heard's school in the village for a short time when they were children, but their parents had been unable to afford the fees for long, even though they were only two pence per week each.

Since coming to these weekly meetings Archie and Bill had learned to read a few simple passages from the bible and John was surprised at the progress they had made and wished he could do the same. Neither of John's friends mentioned his condition to those present at the meeting, for fear of embarrassing him and John, himself, suddenly found he had not thought of his problem the whole evening. He had been so impressed by what had been said, and the friendliness of those who were present, that he decided to come again.

As the three young men walked home John became very quiet while the others talked excitedly about what had been said and done during the evening. Suddenly John said, 'I wish I knew more about the bible. I haven't even got one'. His pals were quiet for a few moments; they were touched by his remark and remembered their own reactions when they first met the Methodist preacher and were introduced to what had now become a wonderful book to them.

Bill was the first to reply to John. 'Be patient, John,' he said, 'it will come to you as it did to us'. Archie promised to do what he could to get a bible for John.

'Thanks Archie,' John replied in a voice that was so much more cheerful. 'I shall look forward to next week'.

By the time he arrived home John was feeling so much better even his father noticed a change in him. He continued to take the potion Mother Mumford had made up for him, regularly, and it seemed to help him. In a few weeks he was again able to visit Jane's home which, along with his weekly meetings, gave him great joy and did much to turn his mind away from his illness and the uncertainty of the future.

During the following summer months Archie and Bill worked long hours and were often unable to attend the Methodist meetings. John came to appreciate what Miss

Trelevan was trying to do for him and she had, by this time, been told of his condition. She created opportunities to be alone with him in order to share his thoughts and help him to come to terms with his illness.

By the end of that summer even Jane began to feel that perhaps John would get well again, despite all she had heard about this terrible disease. Late one evening they were sitting together on the cliffs looking out over the calm waters of the ocean, watching the sun set over the horizon like a fall of fire. All around them the heather and ling stretched like a purple carpet as far as the eye could see. They were enjoying the cool breeze which wafted around their faces after a very hot day. The only sounds were the plaintive cry of a sea parrot to its mate on the big rocks further out to sea. Conversation seemed out of place in such circumstances but at last John broke the silence and shuffled a little closer to Jane and whispered in a husky voice, 'I'm glad I'm getting better, Jane. Wouldn't it be wonderful if we could marry one day?'

Jane was taken by surprise at the mention of marriage and was tongue-tied for a moment. 'Yes, John,' she replied timidly. 'You are so much better than you were a few months ago, aren't you?' But all the while, something seemed to tell her that this was only a temporary remission as had happened with her own mother.

She turned the conversation away from John's illness. 'Did you know that Maria is starting work at the hotel next week?' she said cheerfully. 'Won't it be wonderful for her to be able to find work so near to home?'

Maria was her daughter who was already 12 years old. 'That's good,' John replied. 'It was a lucky day when you came to live here wasn't it'.

They lapsed into silence again, each engrossed in thoughts of the future. The twilight was quickly descending around them and Jane rose to her feet. 'Come on John,' she said firmly. 'It's time you started your journey home'.

'Yes, I think you're right Jane. I feel more tired than usual tonight,' he answered. And standing up he put his arms around her to kiss her goodnight. At this Jane seemed to flinch a little, as she had done on other occasions lately; this puzzled John. He did not know that Jane was fearful of catching his disease through his kisses. She could not bring herself to explain to him but knew that one day she must.

14

Conditions of life for many people in the parish continued to be difficult during the closing years of the 1840's. It took several years to recover from the effects of the corn and potato harvest failures earlier in that decade. Even those farming big acreages, such as James Passmore, found it hard to pay their way, while many smallholders like Jim Foster went out of business. More and more people were seeking Parish relief and many of the labouring classes found it hard to get work. During this time the needs of this latter class of people became so acute that action had to be taken.

A subscription fund was started to buy food and a penny rate was levied which together brought in £119 with which was purchased 2,500 herrings, 122 bushels of peas, 42 bushels of flour, 1 bushel of barley meal and 902lbs of suet as well as coal and other necessary food for young children. The 'Relief' was given mainly to labourers who did not receive Parish help and whose families consisted of four or more. The value each week was about 4s 3d.

Jim lived for his animals on his few acres and supplemented his income by carting stones from a local quarry to repair roads in the area. He had been secretly pleased when the wrecking gang broke up but badly shocked and saddened when he learnt of the death of his friend, Harry Hickman. He had felt terribly guilty at not having gone back to the beach that night after taking his horse home. Maybe, he reasoned, things would have been different if he had been there to help. Like David he had become very depressed and, living alone as he did, he had no-one to whom he could talk.

Jim's wife, who was David Kellaway's sister, had died soon after their marriage several years before but he had managed to cope alone since that time. Unlike many of his contemporaries he did not visit the pubs but enjoyed being with his stock. His hobby was ringing the bells at the parish church which he had done since the age of 15 years and music, which he loved passionately. He had the wonderful gift of being able to play almost anything on his accordian after hearing the tune just once. He also played the violin and was a member of the little group who accompanied the singing in church from their place in the minstrel's gallery in front of the tower archway.

Jim had been so pleased when David joined the ringing team of which he was the captain. They had previously all too rarely met; now they saw each other on practice nights and on Sundays in church. The brothers-in-law had a great deal in common and it was a comfort to Jim to be able to share some of his thoughts with David whom he knew to be a changed man. They even discussed their wrecking experiences and confessed their abhorrence to one another for what they had done in the past. All this was so helpful to Jim and he seemed to blossom into a new man.

It gave Jim great joy to be able to take part in the services of the church, even though he was not so spiritually minded as David. But he loved his music so much that he entered into the spirit of his playing just as if he was a little boy. There was just one thing that troubled him sometimes — and that was the length of the sermons. Hour glasses were quite commonly used in those days to time the sermons. One hour was the usual length of such a discourse at that time when preaching was deemed of more importance than prayer or praise. Such was the occasional enthusiasm of the Revd Chanter that at the end of one hour he would turn the glass, which was fixed on the pulpit, with the remark, 'Let us have another glass, brethren, before we part'. This irritated Jim sometimes because he needed to be with his stock — the feeding of which he had been unable to complete before going to ring the bells.

The ringing team at the parish church was recognised as being of above average ability. They were a faithful group of men who never failed in their duty to call upon the people to worship. From time to time one or two young lads came to learn the art under Jim Foster's instruction. Jim was a strict disciplinarian with his team; he understood the danger that could arise out of a misuse of the bell ropes. The heaviest bell weighed 18 hundredweight and when it was swinging there could be trouble if the rope was not handled carefully.

One autumn evening at their usual practice session, Jim called his team to attention. Of the six men who each held a bell rope in readiness to pull at Jim's command was a recruit who had been learning for several weeks and was in the team for the first time. The bells had already been raised to the upside down position where they rested against a wooden beam called a 'stay' so that a gentle pull on the rope would start them swinging and they would then be controlled by the ringers.

Jim's signal to start ringing was the word 'gone' when he pulled on the rope of the lightest bell which he was to ring, setting it in action while each of the other men did the same in succession. The recruit, a young man called Tom Elliott, was on bell number three and he did very well for several rounds. The swinging of the bell caused the rope to go up and down and, at its lowest level, the ringer was able to take hold of a thickening called a 'fillet' by which he was able to control the striking, as he did again at the end of the rope when the bell swung in the opposite direction and the rope was pulled up through a small hole in the ceiling of the ringing chambers.

The captain was delighted by the way Tom was handling his bell and the thought that one day he would make a good ringer was crossing his mind when, without any warning, the young man had crashed his head against the ceiling and was lying motionless on the floor. The rope was flying around the rest of the team as the bell continued to swing out of control. Jim acted instantly by ordering his team to set their bells up. This took three or four rounds and all the while he knew that he and his men were in danger of having the loose rope flung around their necks and being pulled up to the ceiling. After what seemed an endless time the bells were back in position and Jim rushed to the aid of young Tom and at once realised that he was dead. It seemed that as the bell rope had come down and Tom had caught hold of the fillet, it had somehow tangled around his arm and pulled him violently against the ceiling, fracturing his skull.

Everyone was obviously very shocked at what had happened and, as far as was known, such an accident had never before occurred in that belfry. As captain of the team Jim naturally felt the responsibility most of all and he was grateful for David's sympathy and support. Several weeks passed before they felt able to ring those bells again.

But happier days were not far away. Another Christmas was almost upon them when the ringers, along with the instrumentalists and the choir of the church, would join the staff of the Abbey, along with the estate workers, including David, Archie and Bill, at the annual Christmas party. This was the highlight of the year, to which all looked forward with great pleasure, when the old house which had once been a monastery, echoed to the sound of music and laughter as food was distributed plentifully and drink flowed freely. Jim, as usual, took his accordian to play for the dancing and to accompany the carols, which were sung lustily if not very tunefully, as they had been for generations — many of these being unique to that parish.

It was well after midnight when the proceedings were reluctantly brought to an end. The Vicar proposed a vote of thanks to the Squire, who dutifully responded by thanking his staff for their loyalty during the past year and also the musicians and choir and wished everyone a Happy New Year. Finally Jim struck the chord for the National Anthem in which everyone joined, after which the men pulled their cloth caps down around their ears and the women drew their shawls closer to them as they went out into the cold and darkness of the night to wend their home across a little stream by a narrow bridge and up through the woods to the public road.

Most of the company had already gone when tragedy struck. Quite a lot of cider had been consumed that evening and a few of the men were not too steady on their feet. The bridge that had to be crossed immediately on leaving the house had no side walls and after coming from the bright light inside the darkness seemed more intense for a while.

Jack Sleeman was a mason on the estate who was soon to retire. He had worked there all his life and was known to be a steady and reliable man. He had drunk a little too much that night, more than was his custom, and while crossing the bridge he stepped over the side and hit his head on the bottom of the stream and drowned before anyone could find him in the darkness. This second tragedy within so short a time cast a deep gloom over the little community — everyone respected Jack and were very shocked.

Not long after this sad event, David and Jim were with their teams at Speke's Mill, collecting sand for the estate. This is a little bay about one mile south of the Quay where Alfie Baker and his six donkeys worked. When the tide was out each day Alfie loaded some two hundredweight of sand or gravel into the panniers of each animal, then each in turn would set off alone across the pebbles and rocks, up the two hundred feet cliff path, where it waited for its master and the others to arrive. The sand was then unloaded in a special heap according to its type beside the road from where farmers and others collected it.

David and Jim were sitting on the bank, having their usual morning break of bread and cheese and cold tea, discussing the happenings of the past, when the question of the Methodists arose.

'Archie tells me they are trying to find a bit of land in the village where they can build a Chapel,' David remarked.

'I shouldn't have thought there was enough people going to those meetings to need a special building,' replied Jim. 'Anyway, you know what the Squire thinks about Methodists,' he went on with a twinkle in his eye, 'they won't get much out of him for that purpose.'

David was quiet for a while, as if he was trying to work something out in his mind, then he said, 'Well, after all Jim, Miss Trelevan is getting on in years and I expect they are thinking about the future when they might not have anywhere to meet'.

'I suppose you're right David,' replied Jim. 'Besides, we don't all think alike about ways of worship. Perhaps this is why they don't join with the Independent Chapel in the village'.

'I think the Methodists are nearer to the Church of England than they are to the Independents, Jim,' said David, 'but we shall see'.

There the conversation ended and the men got to their feet to begin loading the sand into their butts.

A few days later the Methodist preacher from Callington came to see Miss Trelevan and was able to join with the others at their weekly meeting. During that evening someone remarked that he had heard of a plot of land in the village belonging to an old gentleman called Thomas Chope who lived at Hescott about two miles away and who might be persuaded to sell it to allow them to build a Chapel.

The next evening the man from Callington and Bill Brown set off for the residence of Mr Chope and found him to be at home. After they had waited a while having been admitted by a servant girl, he came into the room — a jolly, good-natured looking old man, a real English country gentleman type. After the introductions were over the purpose of their visit was explained. The old man responded in a way that was beyond their expectations.

'Chapel!! Chapel!!' he said, looking from one to the other. 'Very good thing, I think. Sal,' he shouted, and a girl appeared in answer to his summons. 'Sal, bring some beer'.

The beer was brought in tankards and, as the old man lifted his to his lips, he said, 'Here's success to your undertaking'.

'What countryman are you?' he asked the

Methodist preacher.

'Cornish,' he replied.

'Cornish! Then you are a Cornish clough, ah! Well, I'm a Devonshire dumpling! Do you know I've had some people enquiring about that bit of land for a Chapel. They call themselves Primitive Methodists. I think most of them came from Wiltshire; they are Wiltshire Moonrakers! But it strikes me they have no money. But what are you?'

'We are Wesleyan-Methodists, Sir, and there is no doubt as to our being able to get a little money for you'.

'No doubt! No doubt!' replied the old gentleman. 'I've heard you are a substantial people. Dr Clarke! Dr Clarke! Let me see, was he not one of your people?'

'He was, Sir,' answered the preacher.

'Yes. I thought so. He was a fine fellow'.

(Dr Adam Clarke was one of the famous early Methodists).

There was silence for a while when the Cornishman took the opportunity to bring back the subject of the plot of land.

'Well, Sir,' he said. 'What about this little plot of land?'

'You shall have it at a yearly rent,' replied the old man.

'We can scarcely build on such conditions. Will you kindly sell us the freehold?'

'No, that I can't do,' he replied. 'You see it is entail property but you shall have any sort of lease that suits you best'.

After a little more talk the kind hearted old gentleman agreed to a lease on the most easy terms. The deed of that lease had only just been completed when the old man died, but his heir took the necessary measures to make the plot strictly the committee's own and the Chapel was eventually built.

15

John Cann's condition had deteriorated during the autumn of that year, so much so that he could no longer walk the three miles to see Jane. Soon after Christmas his boss felt that he was no longer fit to work so, at the end of January, he made his last delivery of bread to the hotel. When he told Jane the sad news that day she was naturally very upset but surprised herself by the way she accepted it. She had felt for several months that this would eventually happen but her sadness was not so much for herself as for John. Her feelings for him had recently become more and more those of a caring friend and any idea of marriage had long since gone. John, on the other hand, still clung to the hope that he might make a full recovery and eventually be able to marry Jane.

After having stopped work for a few days and been able to rest, John felt a little stronger — so much so that he decided to walk to Jane's home one evening. She was very surprised to see him. 'I felt I just had to come, Jane,' he said, almost gasping for breath after his long walk.

Having rested a while he took Jane's hand as they sat together on the settle and looked into her eyes. 'I've had such a queer feeling today Jane,' he said. 'I made myself come here tonight because I felt that I may not see you again'. Then he paused a moment as if too frightened to say what was on his mind. 'I'm not going to die, am I Jane?' he whispered as he held her hand even more tightly.

Jane was very surprised at John's outburst, he had never talked like this before and she could only reply, 'You're very tired after your long walk John. I will make you a cup of tea'.

She deliberately kept the conversation away from his condition for the rest of the evening and long before his usual time to leave she suggested he ought to prepare to go home.

'I will come to the top of the cliff road with you John,' she told him, 'but promise me you will walk home slowly'.

'Yes, I will do that,' he replied weakly. 'I haven't the strength to do anything else'.

So they set off up the hill, with his arm linked in hers, stopping every hundred yards or so for John to recover his breath. Jane did not speak much during that short walk; John's words about dying had touched her deeply because they added weight to her own thoughts that this might be the last time she might see him.

When they reached the cliff top and were on the level road Jane knew that she had to make her farewell quickly before she broke down in tears, which she felt would disturb John. It was a cold night with a strong east wind into which John would have to walk all the way home. As she said goodnight Jane held him in her arms so tightly that John looked into her face as if to say, 'Why is it so different tonight?' He then kissed her on the cheek and, with a final weak hug, he whispered, 'Goodbye, dear Jane, I shall love you always'.

Jane was so overcome that she could only murmur, 'I love you too, John, go carefully won't you'.

She watched his frail, almost ghostly figure disappear into the darkness of the night and longed to go with him but knew that her family awaited her at home. As she started to walk down the hill Jane could stand the strain no longer — she burst into tears, her uncontrollable sobs mingling with the murmur of the waves gently breaking on the beach below. She felt in the depths of her being that John's 'Goodbye' would be very real and that she would not see him again.

Just before midnight two young men were walking home after having spent the evening at the Bear Inn. They were climbing the steep hill into the village where they lived when a break in the clouds allowed the moon to cast its light on the road for a moment. The lads thought they saw a dark shape at the foot of the hedge and, on looking a little more closely, they found it to be the body of a man. Their first thought was that someone had had too much to drink but, as they tried to lift him to his feet, they recognised John Cann whom they knew very well, he being of their age group. It was obvious to them that he was dead and they were badly shocked and hurried into the village to get help. John had found that a combination of a cold east wind and the very steep hill had been too much for him and the effort had brought on a lung haemorrhage from which he had collapsed and died.

It was not until late the following day that Jane heard the tragic news. She was obviously very upset and felt guilty that she had allowed John to walk home alone, but the shock was tempered by the fact that their meeting that evening had convinced her that he had not long to live. As she remembered again that walk up the cliff path and the farewell that followed Jane had no regrets, but was quietly thankful for the happiness their friendship had brought and that John had not lingered on in great distress as she remembered her mother had done.

It was John's father who was the most badly hurt by the tragedy. The young men who found the body naturally went to Mr Cann's home for help. The shock was too much for him, with the result that after the funeral he slipped back into an even worse depressive state. During that time David spent many hours with him and was a great comfort and support — along with Mother Mumford's decoctions.

Miss Trelevan and her little group were also very shocked at John's sudden death. They had come to be very attached to him and he had entered into the spirit of their meetings and had greatly benefited from what he had learned.

For the second time Jane found herself trying to settle down to life after a bereavement but, unlike her struggle after the death of her husband, she was now greatly helped by the fact that she felt so much a part of the hotel and was very appreciative of the kindness of Mr and Mrs Hockin. Her family was fast growing up — her daughter, Maria, being already a popular young lady among the staff and guests in her place of work.

Jane did not have much spare time between her work at the hotel and looking after the children. But a few minutes did sometimes occur, especially in the summer evenings. There was nothing she enjoyed more than sitting in the heather overlooking the little harbour where she and John had so often sat, watching the small boats coming and going. She loved being alone after the rush and bustle of her work and her mind often went back over her life as she realised how conditions for her had changed. She remembered how difficult it had been for her mother to bring up such a large family while, at the same time, being such a sick woman. Then she thought of Harry and herself in their struggle to feed and clothe their family; but amidst these unhappy memories many pleasant experiences came to her mind which she would not have missed for anything. Even in Harry's tragic death and later when John died, Jane was now able to recall these events in a positive manner, looking to the future with much more confidence than she had ever done before.

During her childhood days Jane had occasionally gone to Church, but it was not until she started work at the Abbey that she attended regularly. Then the Squire and his family occupied their own little chapel in the parish church week by week, while the staff were expected to be there each Sunday morning in a pew allotted to them quite close to the family. There they were expected to behave with dignity with the Squire's eye firmly fixed upon them. They had to file out of the church about half an hour before the service ended in order to return to the Abbey to prepare lunch by the time the family returned.

Although the services did not mean much to Jane at that time, some of the things she remembered seemed to have a connection with her deeper thoughts while sitting alone on those cliffs. It was as if the beauty that was all about her on those lovely summer evenings and for which she was so grateful was all part of the acts of worship in which she had taken part so often in the past, but much more wonderful.

Jane felt an urge to share these thoughts with someone. She knew it ought to be the Vicar but that was something she knew she could not bring herself to do. One evening as she sat in her favourite spot the idea of talking to her cousin David suddenly came to her mind. So when he next went to visit her he was quite unprepared for what was to come. He hardly had time to sit down before Jane started to question him. The result was an inspiring evening from which David received as much satisfaction from sharing her thoughts as she did in listening to his replies to her questions.

134

16

Later on in that same summer Jane was again sitting in her favourite spot on the cliffs, just before the sun disappeared below the horizon. The air was warm and balmy after a very hot day and the flat calm sea was shimmering like a giant silver carpet in the dying rays. She was so engrossed in the wonderful spectacle before her that she did not notice a man step off a small yacht moored to the quay and start to walk up the path leading to the hotel, which would bring him past where she was sitting. It was not until he was almost abreast of her that she turned with a start, the beauty of that wonderful scene still reflecting in her eyes and face.

'Excuse me,' said the man, 'I think I have seen you before somewhere'.

Jane got up quickly, though rather awkwardly, and gave a little curtsey. 'I'm sorry sir,' she replied, 'I can't remember'.

The young man was of military appearance and his voice gave the impression that he was used to giving orders to others.

'Did you ever work at the Abbey?' he

asked, a little more gently this time as he noticed how Jane seemed to recoil at his tone of voice.

'Yes sir,' she answered timidly, 'I was there for several years'.

Then, in a flash, she remembered the teenager who came to stay sometimes and who often teased her and sometimes made passes at her when they happened to be alone. Jane blushed deeply as she remembered all this and the wry smile on the man's face gave her the impression that he was thinking her thoughts too.

'I thought I remembered you,' he continued. 'You haven't changed a bit, just as lovely as when you were 18,' and he grinned mischievously. Jane could no longer look into his face but turned her eyes to the ground.

'Care for a trip around the Point one day in my little cockle shell?' he suggested with a twinkle in his eyes as he pointed down to the harbour.

'Oh no sir, thank you, I couldn't do that,' she replied with a distinct nervousness in her voice. 'I've never been in a boat,' and she made as if to brush past him in the narrow path leading to her cottage when Mr Hockin appeared. He looked from one to the other as if sensing there was something wrong between them and then began to talk to the man.

Jane rushed home and flopped into the settle feeling frightened and exhausted; she had not expected such a traumatic end to such a lovely evening. But after thinking about the incident for a few minutes she realised that she might have made something out of the conversation that had not been intended by the man; perhaps his motives were quite genuine and that it was just his manner of conversation.

When Jane went to work the next morning she was met by Mrs Hockin. 'What happened last night?' she asked. 'My husband was very concerned about you, you looked so frightened when he met you coming up the cliff path'.

'I think I was being a bit silly,' replied Jane. 'I have thought a lot about it since and I don't think the man meant any harm'.

'I'm sure he didn't Jane,' Mrs Hockin assured her, 'I know him well; he's a very nice young man'. Then she went on to tell Jane that he was a typical young naval officer who had been promoted quickly since qualifying at the Naval College where he had been when Jane first met him at the Abbey. She felt a tingle of pride when she heard all this.

'Do you think he really meant what he said about taking me out in his yacht?' she asked shyly.

'Yes, I'm sure he did,' replied her mistress.

Jane was not so sure and felt she would need a lot of persuading before she could do such a thing.

But all this was forgotten when just two weeks later Frank Hockin became ill and died only a few days after his fortieth birthday. He had been greatly worried a few years earlier when the pier-head had collapsed during a terrible storm. He had had the difficult task of getting it rebuilt, while at the same time, trying to carry on the business of the port which, at that time, was considerable.

Mrs Hockin found Jane to be a great comfort at the time of her bereavement — she seemed to know just how she felt and said the right things at the right time. So it was with much sadness that the two women had to say farewell when Mrs Hockin went to live at her old home in Bristol. They had built up a wonderful relationship and Jane felt that she would be forever grateful to her mistress for all her kindness to her and her family.

It was now 1846 and a new tenant of the hotel and harbour had been appointed by the Squire. He was Daniel Carter, a locally born man who had lived away from the parish for several years and had qualified as a surgeon, a very unusual achievement at that time. He and his wife Ellen had a very young daughter and it was not long before Maria, Jane's elder daughter, was appointed nursemaid to the child — a job she enjoyed so much, having looked after small children from a very early age.

Dr Carter soon became deeply involved in the trading life of the little port — both with his own vessels, the 'Arrowhead' and 'Rapide' and especially in bringing in material for the restoration of the Parish Church which was taking place at that time. His wife and Jane quickly developed a happy relationship — the latter being able to draw on her experiences in working at the hotel, so helping Ellen who knew very little about that work. A good working team was soon established — Daniel Carter himself being keen to develop the hotel side of his business.

The arrival of the Carter family changed Jane's life a great deal. She found herself talking to her mistress in a way she had never thought to be possible. No longer was she afraid to express her thoughts; in fact, Ellen encouraged her to share her ideas. Gone was the strict mistress-servant relationship she had known all her life and, in its place, there was a woman to woman rapport which brought out the best in Jane. She used what little spare time she had to learn to read and write with Ellen's help and Ellen found herself answering endless questions which Jane put to her about the world outside the small area in which she had lived.

One afternoon when things were a little quieter than usual in the hotel Jane took Ellen to her favourite spot on the cliff overlooking the little harbour. It was a glorious early summer day with the heat of the sun tempered by a gentle breeze off the sea. The two women sat in silence for a while, enjoying the peaceful scene below them with only the sound of the waves gently lapping against the breakwater. A year had passed since the young naval officer had come ashore from his little yacht and Jane had almost forgotten the incident. But in those identical conditions she remembered again and blushed as his words seemed to ring in her ears. Then she went on to tell Ellen what happened that evening.

'What a thrill you must have had, Jane,' she said, her eyes shining at the thought of such a trip. 'I don't seem to have such excitements in my life', she added.

'I'm afraid I didn't see it that way,' Jane replied. 'I was a bit scared, I can tell you'.

'Would you go if he offered you the chance again?' asked Ellen.

Jane was silent for a moment. 'I would if there were other people on board,' she answered, as if she couldn't believe what she was saying. 'But I don't suppose the chance will come again,' she said with a note of sadness in her voice. The two women went on to talk about their own lives, sharing in each other's family problems, and all too soon it was time to go back to the hotel to get on with the evening work.

Jane's two elder boys were now aged 12 and 13 years and they were anxious to start work. Frank, the younger, had come to love the sea since the family moved to their little cottage and he spent his days in and out of the boats moored at the quay and watching the men working in them. He had been fascinated to see how they hobbled small sailing craft out of the harbour with rowing boats and he had often gone with them when the weather was fine.

Frank decided that this was the work he wanted to do so his mother had a talk with Dr Carter who agreed to employ Frank to help wherever he was needed. His work was mainly with the boats but he also attended to the needs of the men working in the lime kilns, keeping them supplied with ale in their hot and dusty work. It was a comfort to Jane to know that the lad was happy in his work and that she was able to keep a watchful eye on him. Nevertheless she was rather concerned that he would be involved in hobbling boats out the harbour because, only a few years before the family moved to their present home, a rowing boat had capsized and three men were drowned during such an operation.

Unlike his brother, Jane's elder son was a quiet, shy lad who was not at all attracted to the sea. He loved animals and had often said he would like to work on a farm as his father had done. His mother wondered if Mr Passmore would employ her son and perhaps even allow him to live in the house with the family, as often happens on farms — it would be too far for the lad to walk to work each day. So Jane decided to ask her mistress to give her a free afternoon in order that she may walk up to the farm and talk with her old employers.

This was to be a sentimental journey for Jane — not having been back to the old home since the family moved three years before — and she wondered what her feelings would be. It was a lovely autumn day on which she chose to visit the Passmores and as she walked along the lane leading to the farm a strange sensation crept over her. Everything she saw reminded her of days long past — the hedges and trees, the turn in the lane where she again saw the chimney of her old home above the hedge; the well from which had been drawn so many buckets of water. Jane stopped there for a while and remembered that moment when George Arnold had surprised her as she was pulling up a bucket of water. She seemed to be reliving that meeting as she gazed down at the well and it was as if she could hear George's voice again as clearly as if he had been at her side. A wonderful joy swept through her — it was as if that memory had grown into something so much deeper, so much more meaningful than she had known it before. In fact, it was for her no longer just a memory but a present reality — she knew at that moment that her feelings for George had developed into such a longing to be with him that it seemed to overwhelm her.

It was then that Jane realised how much she herself had changed. The three years work at the hotel had brought about a self-confidence she had not thought possible. Jane pondered on all this as she continued her walk until she reached her old home. Here she allowed a little sentimentality to intrude into her thoughts as she stood gazing at the old cottage, remembering so many things that had happened there from the day she married Harry. But it was on a note of thankfulness that she walked into the farmyard. There she met Farmer Passmore, just as she remembered she had done when she went to tell him of Harry's death.

'Hullo Jane,' he exclaimed with a note of excitement in his voice, 'what brings you here?' Jane had seen the Passmores on two or three occasions since leaving their employment when they came down to the hotel pub but had not been able to have a conversation with them.

'I would like to have a chat with you and your wife, Mr Passmore, if you have the time,' she replied.

'Why yes, of course, come in Jane, my wife will be delighted to see you'. They walked into the kitchen where Mrs Passmore greeted Jane warmly and set about making her a cup of tea. They talked about her work and life at the hotel for some time until, during a break in the conversation, Jane looked at Mr Passmore and asked:

'Could you do with some help on the farm?'

The farmer was a little surprised at such a question from Jane — not thinking she was speaking about one of her boys, as he had not realised they were old enough to start work.

'What sort of work were you thinking about, Jane?' he asked.

'Oh, its not for me, Mr Passmore,' she replied hastily. 'Jamie is 13 years old now and he would like to work on a farm'.

'How quickly the children seem to grow up,' Mrs Passmore interrupted, with a glance at her husband. 'It seems only a short time ago that they were babies at the cottage'.

They went on to discuss the question further and to Jane's surprise and delight the idea was accepted with enthusiasm by her friends. The Passmores had no children and the thought of having a 13 year old living with them and working on the farm appealed to them.

In those days children from poor families were often apprenticed to farmers and, in many instances, were badly treated. Many masters and mistresses were kind enough to the children in their care but the system gave no encouragement to others to be considerate. In consequence these were badly clothed, underfed and overworked — some as young as 9 years. It was quite common for a fried egg to be shared between two children.

Jane knew of such children and as she walked home that afternoon her heart was filled with thankfulness that her boys would be freed from such an ordeal. It was agreed that Jamie should start work on Michaelmas Day which was just two weeks away. So on the previous evening Jane had the sad task of preparing for the flight of one of her little birds from the family nest. It took all the courage she could muster to withhold her tears as she packed the few items of clothing into a little bundle for her son Jamie to take with him to his place of work.

Jane was up quite early the next morning to see young Frank off to work at the harbour. He would still be living at home and she knew that she would see him around sometimes during the day. But she felt as if she was losing Jamie, knowing that she might not see him again for several weeks. Mrs Carter had given her time off from work that day to take her son to the farm so they set off together with the lad carrying his bundle of clothes across his shoulder.

James was even more subdued than usual as they made their way along the lane and, as they passed their old home, it seemed to Jane as if it was only yesterday that the boys had been toddlers, playing outside the cottage. Coming into the farmyard, Jane glanced down at her son and saw his sad little eyes fixed on her; then he put his hand into hers and a faint smile spread across his face as if he was trying to comfort his mother. It was with the utmost difficulty that Jane withheld her tears which she knew she must do for Jamie's sake.

At that moment Mrs Passmore appeared at the back door of the farmhouse with a welcoming smile and all their sadness was forgotten as she explained, 'Hullo Jamie. My! how you've grown'. The lad seemed to be lost for words but then Mr Passmore came along and he seemed to relax at once when his new boss started to talk about the work he would be doing. After a cup of tea the two of them went off together with just a backward glance from Jamie to his mother as he went out, but that look meant so much to Jane for it seemed to gather up all the love and care she had been privileged to give to that young life.

Jane felt much happier when she left for home after a long talk with Mrs Passmore, who was so kind and understanding; she felt sure that her son would be well looked after.

It was as if she had found a new sense of freedom as she tripped lightly down the lane towards her home. She was so thankful that her boys were starting the work they wanted to do.

17

There had been a great deal of sickness in the parish following the years of the hungry forties, about which Dr Carter felt very concerned. Although he had given up his work as a surgeon to take over the little hotel and harbour, he still yearned to get involved again in his work of healing. He had been able to help quite often when ships had been wrecked and seamen had been injured since he came to that area.

Very few yachts and other small craft came into the harbour during the winter months, which made for far less work in the house and he himself had less to do in management. So after much discussion with his wife he decided to buy a small dilapidated house in the village and make it a fit place in which to see people who were in need of his help. Mother Mumford was getting very frail and unable to continue helping people, as she had done for more than 40 years. She had been a great blessing to so many people during that time when no other help was available. She was known and loved by everyone and when she eventually died the whole population of the parish mourned her passing.

When the house was ready Daniel Carter decided to use it on two mornings of each week but he soon discovered that the demand for his services was so great that he increased it to three mornings. After the first two or three weeks he realised that he needed help with the patients before they went in to see him, so as he drove home one day the idea came to him that perhaps Jane might be able to join him. Just before she went home that evening he met her in the kitchen.

'Oh, Jane,' he said, 'I've got an idea I would like to put to you'.

Jane turned with a look of surprise in her eyes. 'Yes Sir,' she replied, looking from the doctor to her mistress.

'I wonder if you would like to help me in my surgery,' he went on. 'I need someone to look after the patients before they come in to see me'.

But even before he had finished speaking Jane was holding her face in her hands. 'Oh no, Sir,' she replied, with a note of fear in her voice. 'I don't think I could do that'.

'I think you could, Jane,' the doctor continued encouragingly. 'You are just the person to comfort and support anyone who is waiting to see me'.

The idea seemed a little less frightening to Jane now than when the doctor first suggested it. She had had visions of being involved in blood-letting and all kinds of horrible things.

'Will you please let me think about it Sir?' she replied. 'I will tell you in the morning'.

'All right Jane,' answered Doctor Carter. 'But please don't worry about it. I'm sure you would enjoy the work'.

That evening Jane pondered over the doctor's suggestion as she sat alone in her home. The more she thought about it the more attractive the idea seemed to become. She thought of all the people she would meet — many of whom would be known to her — but whom she did not see very often. Since working at the hotel she had come to enjoy meeting people and felt so much more at ease with them than in former years.

It was a very cheerful Jane who confronted Doctor Carter the next morning. 'I'd love to help you, Sir,' she said confidently.

'Good. That's fine, Jane,' he replied. 'You can come with me tomorrow'.

Immediately after breakfast the next morning Doctor Carter set off for the village and his surgery with Jane proudly seated beside him in the little dog-cart pulled by a pony which he had lately acquired to help transport the family. There were very few wheeled vehicles in that area at that time and the local people just gazed in astonishment at the sight of the doctor and Jane bumping along the rough road. From time to time a man would touch his cap and a woman would give a little curtsey — all of which was very embarrassing to Jane.

It was not long before the people of the village and beyond heard of the help Daniel Carter was offering and Jane was kept busy in the waiting room preparing them for their interview with him — all of which must have been quite an experience for them, not having ever seen a doctor before. All the help they had ever received for their sicknesses had been that which Mother Mumford had been able to offer them. Jane was also responsible for collecting the few pence that Doctor Carter charged each patient for the various decoctions he gave them and which he obtained from an apothecary at Bideford. She quickly settled into her new work and found great satisfaction in talking to people about their problems. She looked forward to the surgery mornings and enjoyed the ride into the village.

The summer of 1853 had been gloriously

hot and Jane was taking her usual walk down the cliff path one evening after finishing work when again she met the young naval officer who had spoken to her some two years before and when she had been so embarrassed. This time she felt relaxed and at ease as he spoke to her.

'Good evening,' he said cheerfully. 'How nice to see you again'.

'Good evening, Sir,' Jane replied in a confident tone with a little curtsey, acknowledging her station in life.

'Do you still work here?' he went on with the same twinkle in his eyes that Jane had noticed when last they met.

'Oh yes, Sir,' she said 'and I like it very much'. The details of their last meeting suddenly flashed through her mind when the man had suggested that she might like a trip in his yacht. She secretly hoped he would not repeat that offer but she was to be disappointed.

'You're called Jane, aren't you?' he queried with a slight frown.

'That's right, Sir,' Jane replied, bracing herself for what he might say next.

'I've still got my little boat as you can see', pointing down to the harbour where the yacht was moored at the quay. 'Do you remember how I offered you a trip along the coast when I was staying here a year or two ago?'

'Yes Sir, I do,' replied Jane with as much enthusiasm as she could muster.

'I think you were a bit frightened at the idea then, weren't you?'

'Yes, Sir, I was,' Jane admitted. 'I didn't want to go alone'.

The young man's bronzed face wreathed in smiles and Jane saw the same mischievous look in his eyes as she had often seen all those years before when he stayed at the Abbey where she was working.

'I don't think you need be afraid of me,' he replied with a chuckle. 'You didn't give me time to explain what I thought of doing'. Then he went on to say how kind everyone had been whenever he had stayed at the hotel and he thought that two or three of them might like to come with him for a trip across the bay to Ilfracombe and back one day when the weather was good.

This idea seemed to be much more acceptable to Jane than that of going alone and the officer noticed the change of attitude in her eyes and said, 'I will talk to your employer about it and hear what he thinks'.

The young man then went on up the path to the hotel while Jane settled into her favourite spot among the heather to watch the sun set in its usual beauty.

The next morning Ellen Carter met Jane when she came to work and seemed to be quite excited. She and her husband had had a talk with the officer and it was agreed that she and Jane and young Maria should go with him the next day while the weather was good. It was not Jane's day to accompany the doctor to the surgery and they were not very busy at the hotel, so it was thought to be a good opportunity to have a nice day out before the winter set in. But it was obvious that Jane was not able to share the enthusiasm of Mrs Carter and Maria.

It was high tide at 9.00am that morning which was the last day of September. Everyone was on the quay, ready to step aboard the little yacht whose paintwork gleamed in the morning sun. The day promised to be fine and warm — a repeat of so many during past weeks. Jane's younger son, Frank, and two other men were waiting in a rowing boat to hobble the yacht out of the harbour to the open sea. Jane felt proud to see Frank enjoying his work alongside the adults and when they were clear of the harbour and the yacht's sails had been hoisted she and Maria waved him goodbye.

Jane was glad that Ellen Carter was with

her because she was the best able to talk to their host whose name she discovered was Alex Simpson and whom she found to be a charming host. They soon settled down in their seats in the little wheelhouse as the yacht skimmed across the water before the fresh westerly wind. Jane and Maria had never been at sea before and although they felt a little uncomfortable they were soon enjoying the view of the coast and their home. Alex Simpson's constant chatter kept their minds occupied as he pointed out various landmarks on their starboard side which were well known to them while, on the port side, the morning sun showed up Lundy Island in all its beauty.

The skipper decided to keep close to land around Bideford Bay instead of going straight across to Ilfracombe in order that his guests might get a better view of the villages along the coast. This they much enjoyed because he seemed to know so much about the area and kept up a constant commentary. As they headed north after surveying the bay and getting away from the shelter of the land the wind began to freshen so much so that Alex had to take in some sail. The sea, too, was getting a little choppy which made things more uncomfortable for his guests. At about mid-day they tied up at Ilfracombe pier and went ashore for some refreshments. The ladies enjoyed all this very much, especially Jane and Maria for whom it was a wonderful experience after their very hum-drum way of life. They spent a little time looking around the shops until Alex Simpson suggested that they should get back to the yacht.

It was Ellen who noticed that he was looking rather anxiously at the sky. 'Is there something wrong, Alex?' she asked when they were at a little distance from the others.

'Oh, no, there's nothing wrong,' he replied, almost casually. 'But I think we ought to be setting off in case the wind should strengthen; I don't want to miss the tide back at your home'.

They quickly got on board and slipped out of the harbour without any trouble. But after only a short time on the open sea they realised they were in for an uncomfortable trip home. The wind had strengthened considerably and was backing towards the southwest, while the sea was becoming more rough as the minutes passed. At one time the skipper considered the possibility of returning to the harbour but decided to continue the voyage believing that the wind would soon abate.

The women were becoming more and more anxious, especially Jane and Maria. From time to time Ellen caught a glimpse of Alex Simpson's eyes as he struggled to tack into the wind with his mainsail and bowsprit furled and flapping uselessly against the mast and she realised that he was becoming very concerned for their safety. He had not reckoned, when setting out, on the risk of a gale suddenly blowing up in that area without warning, at the time of the Autumnal Equinox, but he knew that they often died out as quickly as they arose.

They had not gone far when the skipper came to the conclusion that they could not possibly reach their destination while the gale continued with such force and, anyway, he reasoned, he would be unable to get his little craft into the harbour; the risk of being blown on to the rocks surrounding it was too great. He decided to head for Lundy Roads where he could find shelter from the wind; then the problem arose that the women's relatives would be very worried when they did not reach home on the evening tide but this, he felt, was the lesser of the two risks he had to take.

Alex tried to talk to his friends about his plans, as well as he was able above the roar of wind and sea; he also tried to comfort them because by now they all realised they were in some trouble and were also very seasick. He had to use all his expertise to keep his yacht head on into the wind and then to tack, first to the north and then to the south. He could see Lundy in the distance but seemed to be making little progress towards the island.

The little party's spirits were by this time very low; conversation was impossible and each was left with her own thoughts and fears. A depression had settled over them. Maria was reduced to tears and was very frightened. Her mother, who was sitting on the opposite side of the wheelhouse to her daughter, got up and crossed over in order to sit beside her and comfort her; at this moment the yacht rolled off an extra large wave which sent Jane crashing against the wheel and knocking her head on the instrument panel. Ellen acted immediately and signalled to Alex to stay at the controls while she lifted Jane on to a seat but found her to be unconscious — just temporarily concussed she thought — so she held her in her arms.

This spurred the skipper into action. He had noticed what he thought to be a coaster running before the wind on his port beam, between the island and the mainland. Realising that he had to get immediate help for Jane he hoisted a distress signal and hoped that the lookout on the vessel would see it.

He hoped to be able to transfer his injured friend to the coaster in order that she might receive the necessary medical help as soon as possible.

He had not long to wait: almost immediately he noticed the vessel had altered course and was approaching him from the windward side so as to shelter the yacht. During this time Alex had managed to tell Ellen what he had decided to do and she agreed with him. She, in turn, passed on the message to Maria who was by now even more distressed and she pleaded with Ellen to let her go with her mother. Her mistress could see that she would have to be very firm about this and, in spite of Maria's almost hysterical outbursts, she had to refuse. It distressed Ellen that because of the noise around them she was not able to explain her reasons in a quiet manner.

The coaster was now almost within hailing distance but because of the conditions was not sure if he would be able to make his requests known to the skipper. But as soon as she came directly to windward the sea and the wind seemed to quieten considerably as the vessel, which was in ballast, was high in the water and provided a wonderful shelter for the little yacht.

Almost immediately there was a shout

from the coaster: 'What can I do for you?'

Alex grabbed his loud hailer and replied, 'Can you take an injured woman aboard?'

'Yes,' came back the reply. 'Have you a stretcher on board?'

'No,' answered Alex who could see the crew of the vessel already preparing to throw a rope to his yacht in order to keep her as close to their vessel as possible in the difficult conditions.

Alex had by now lashed his helm and when the rope came across he secured it firmly to his capstan; after this he gave the signal that he was ready to receive the stretcher. In a very short while a member of the crew was sliding down the rope with a stretcher lashed to his back. After greeting Alex and explaining that they were bound for Barry he lost no time in helping to lift Jane, who was still unconscious, on to the stretcher. She was securely fastened and, with another line attached, she was slowly pulled by the crew up the side of the heaving ship but, just after she had been lifted clear of the yacht's rail, the two vessels seemed to sink into a trough in the swell at the same time, causing Jane to touch the water for a few seconds and thus become very wet. Fortunately the weather had been so hot that summer and the temperature of the sea was equally high so that she was not likely to suffer any ill effects.

The rescue was completed, with Jane safely aboard the coaster along with the crewman, who had been thanked by Alex and requested to convey the thanks of his guests and himself to his skipper. After being dried as well as was possible Jane was placed, still unconscious, on a bunk in the captain's cabin; then, after farewell exchanges, the coaster moved off towards her destination, leaving Alex and his friends to face again the full force of the gale.

The two women seemed to be stunned after all that had happened in so short a time; it was like a bad dream to them. For Alex, however, there was still the reality of having to get his yacht into calmer waters. Slowly but surely they crept towards the island until at last they began to feel that the high cliffs were breaking some of the force of the wind and, eventually, the sea too became less rough. But at last the struggle was over and they were anchored within a few hundred yards of land which, for them, seemed like another world.

No-one had tried to speak since the coaster set off with Jane aboard but now they could talk in peace. It was Alex who started the conversation when he said, 'I'm sorry my friends for all the worry I have caused you on this trip'.

'There is no need to apologise, Alex,' Ellen replied. 'No-one was expecting such a gale to blow up. We can only hope that Jane will soon be well enough to come home. What are your plans for us now?' she continued.

'We shall have to stay here tonight, Ellen,' Alex explained, 'and hope that conditions will have improved by morning to allow us to catch the first high tide'.

Maria was greatly distressed about her mother but Ellen was a wonderful comfort to her. 'Come on Maria,' she said, 'let's have a cup of tea'.

Alex had thoughtfully brought the necessary provisions for his guests so Ellen set about preparing a little meal while Alex looked around the yacht to make sure all was well after the terrible battering it had received while crossing the bay. Neither of the women felt like eating much after their bout of seasickness but they enjoyed their cup of tea while they talked of their plans for sleeping that night. It was arranged that Ellen and Maria should share the main cabin, while Alex said he would manage in the tiny single one.

The cloud was gradually clearing from the west as the evening progressed and the sun dropped behind the island, extending the shadows of the high cliffs across the yacht. The little party sat in the twilight as their boat rose and fell on the ocean swell, each reliving the terrifying experiences of the trip that had begun in such a cheerful, carefree manner. Their thoughts were with Jane and how she was being cared for and with their families at home as they wondered what had happened when they did not return on the evening tide. Alex explained to the women that they would not be expected that night with such a gale sweeping the area. With these thoughts they finally settled down for the night, knowing that they would have to make an early start in the morning in order to catch the high tide at ten o'clock, with the hope that the weather would have improved.

The next day dawned bright and clear. The wind had dropped considerably and veered to the north west, while the sea, although still choppy, was not likely to cause any difficulty for the yacht. After breakfast they weighed anchor and set course for home with thankfulness that the conditions were such that they would be able to catch the tide. After passing through Harty Race, the sea became even calmer, and as they approached the harbour they could see a rowing boat just leaving. The yacht had been sighted earlier as she left Lundy Roads and the men, including Jane's son, had come out to hobble her into port.

There was an anxious moment when contact was first made with the rowing boat, as young Frank looked up at the yacht to see his sister, but not his mother. Alex was watching him closely and knew what must be going through his mind. As soon as they had tied up and stepped on the quay they were greeted by the whole community living there, who had waited so anxiously for their safe return. In a few words Alex explained what had happened and where Jane had been taken; after this Doctor Carter invited everyone into the hotel for refreshments. Here he explained that they had not been so worried as Alex and his friends feared they would be, because during the previous evening someone had been on the cliffs facing Lundy and had seen a boat which they took to be the yacht, entering into the shelter of the island. The two families had, therefore, spent a far less troubled night than their relatives on the yacht had thought possible.

18

The captain of the coaster had been unable to leave the bridge of his vessel while Jane was being transferred from the yacht. But as soon as he had set course again for Barry he left his mate in charge and went below to see his unexpected passenger. He had not been told her name — only the place from which she had set sail that morning and that she was unconscious. He opened the cabin door and approached the bunk quietly to make sure she was breathing normally.

As he stood looking down at the pale figure covered with a blanket a strange feeling crept over him that he was to remember all his life. He could not see her face very clearly in the dim light of the cabin, but as he watched he felt he was in the presence of someone he knew.

After a minute or so Jane began to stir and then opened her eyes and met those of Captain George Arnold. At first George could not speak — it seemed to him as if he was dreaming. But he quickly pulled himself together and, bending low over her, he whispered, 'Is it really you, Jane?' A light of recognition came into her eyes and a flicker of a smile passed her lips before she again lapsed into unconsciousness.

George could hardly believe his eyes as he stood there watching Jane. Was it really the Jane that he had thought so much about during the past years? The Jane whom he had secretly loved for so long? But what was she doing on that yacht? He longed to know the whole story. As he went to the door to leave the cabin George glanced back at Jane and felt compelled to return to the bunk to make sure she was alright; as he bent over her again he kissed her on the cheek. A feeling of guilt swept over him but he had no time to dwell on that — he had to act quickly. His first priority was to get Jane safely ashore where she could receive the necessary treatment. His ship was by now at the entrance to Barry harbour and he was needed on the bridge from where he safely directed the coaster into her berth and from where he was able to make arrangements for Jane to be brought ashore.

Jane was taken to a new Infirmary that had just been built where a doctor examined her and found nothing more serious than concussion and suggested that she should remain there for two days or so. She regained consciousness later that evening and was naturally very upset to find herself so far from home. She was told only that she had been brought into the port on a coaster after being transferred from a yacht where she had been injured. But gradually the events of that day with Ellen and Maria on Alex's yacht became clearer in her mind. She then began to worry about them and what had happened in that terrible gale. Did they get home safely? She became very concerned about how she would find her way home and did her family know where she was? She had never been so far from home before and amongst complete strangers.

She had a terrible headache that evening and she lay on her bed with her eyes closed. She did not hear the door open and footsteps crossing the room but when a voice whispered, 'Are you asleep Jane?' and a hand was laid gently upon hers she opened her eyes with a look of fear in them. It took her a few moments to realise who it was looking down at her; she had not remembered George coming into the cabin of his ship but, in a flash, everything seemed to come alive for Jane and she held up her arms and burst into tears as she held George closely to her. All she could say between her sobs was, 'Oh George, how did you know I was here?'

George did not speak for several minutes but when Jane had dried her tears she was able to tell him all that had happened before her accident and then he filled in his part of the story from the time she was taken aboard his ship. George now realised that Jane was tiring and that he must not talk any longer that evening.

'I'll come in again tomorrow evening,' he said as he prepared to leave her, 'then we can talk about how to get you home'. As he stooped to kiss her goodbye Jane looked up at him with tired eyes. 'This is all true, George, isn't it?' she whispered. 'Tell me that it is not just a dream'.

George felt a lump come into his throat as he knelt beside her bed and held her in his arms. 'It's all very real, Jane dear,' he said hoarsely, 'and we are together at last'.

He turned at the door to take a last look at Jane and he saw, as it were, a light shining in her face — she seemed so radiantly happy.

'Have a good night's sleep,' he said cheerfully. 'I'll be with you tomorrow evening'.

George's life was turned upside down from that time and he knew it would never be the same again. He went back to his bachelor home which was just a few hundred yards from the Infirmary and sank into a chair where he tried to assess the situation. It was long after midnight when at last he went to bed to a restless night.

He knew that his priority was to get Jane safely to her home and family. But how? He realised that he could not let her travel that long journey alone — she had never done such a thing before. The ideal plan would be for him to take a few days leave, but would the company grant him that? But George need not have worried. It was not until he went to the company's office the next morning that he realised how wonderfully well things were beginning to work out for Jane and himself. He was told by his boss that he was to take a cargo of coal to Bideford in two days' time. George could hardly believe what he was hearing — what a great opportunity it would be to get Jane home, he thought; at once he talked to his superior about his problem and he, in turn, said that he had no objections to him taking Jane on board for that short trip.

George went back to the Infirmary with a very light heart that evening. For the first time in his life he felt he really had someone to whom he could give himself, someone for whose welfare he could be concerned. Jane was sitting in a chair in her room when he arrived and she noticed a new lightness in his step as he tripped across the room and how his eyes shone as he greeted her. She held him away at arm's length for a moment, as if to examine his face. 'Whatever has happened, George?' she said. 'You seem so different tonight'.

He was too embarrassed to answer at once but went on to tell Jane about the arrangements he had made with his boss for her return home. Jane's eyes lighted up at the thought of being able to get home so easily — she had been wondering all day about her children and how Maria was coping with the youngest child. Then her cheerfulness suddenly changed to a more serious appearance. 'The doctor says I can leave here tomorrow,' she said, looking across at George. 'Where can I go until your boat leaves?'

George had not expected that problem and he was silent for a few moments. 'I know what you can do, Jane,' he said at last. 'Why not come to my house? It will only be for one night'.

Jane suddenly became very quiet and looked down on the floor. 'Please don't be upset Jane,' he quickly assured her. 'You will be alright with me, there are two bedrooms'. So it was arranged that George should come back to the Infirmary the next afternoon, to take Jane to his home for the night before leaving on his ship the following day.

When Jane was alone after George had gone home she spent a long while thinking about what the morrow would bring. She was quite excited at the thought of being with her loved ones again, but a little apprehensive at the idea of staying at George's home. She was sure he was a good man whom she had come to love, in a way she had not known love before. She felt secure in his presence as if she had known him for many years.

George, too, was thrilled at the idea of Jane sharing his home and looked forward to being able to talk to her about so many things without interruption. He wasted no time after leaving work the next day to collect Jane and walk the short distance to his house. She was still rather unsteady on her feet and although her headache was much better than on the previous day it had not gone completely.

They had a wonderful evening together and often during that time Jane's thoughts went back to her life with Harry in their little cottage on the farm where conditions were often so difficult and when she sometimes had to live on very little food in order that the children had enough.

Jane quietly compared her home with the

one in which she was now sitting, where there seemed to be so many things that she had only dreamed of possessing but which would make life so much more comfortable. But Jane felt that she would not like to live in that house with all the noise and bustle around her — she still preferred the peace and quiet in which she had always lived, despite the many material possessions she lacked.

Late in the evening after they had had a meal George became very quiet, as if he was deep in thought. This troubled Jane because he looked so serious as if he was struggling with a problem. Then he rose from his chair and sat beside Jane on the settee. But before she had time to think what was happening he had taken her hands in his and was looking into her eyes. 'I'm not a twenty year old, Jane,' he said. 'Neither are you. But could you bring yourself to agree to marry me?'

The thought of marriage had crossed Jane's mind the day before when George had held her in his arms at the Infirmary, but she had dismissed it as not being for her, even though she knew she loved him. Now she felt her cheeks burning and knew she was blushing as she so often did in his presence. 'I do love you, George,' she shyly admitted. 'But I don't think I could give up my home and live here; I'm not used to this way of life and, besides, I have my family to think about'.

It was as if George had expected this kind of answer to his question. 'I'm due to retire next year, Jane, and I'd gladly come to live in your area,' he said. 'Perhaps I could find some work at the harbour'.

Jane was silent and again fixed her eyes on the floor. She had not expected to be challenged so suddenly. So many things raced through her mind. She realised that she would soon be alone in her home, her youngest child would be looking to start work. The idea of sharing her home with George appealed to her; she longed for the security he could give her and she felt sure that he was a sincere man who would bring joy into her latter years.

George did not wish to rush Jane into an answer and he realised how much her life would be changed if she accepted his offer. After what seemed a very long time to him she raised her eyes and George saw in them the answer for which he had hoped.

'Yes, George,' she replied, throwing herself into his arms, 'I will marry you'. They both remained silent for several minutes, each too embarrassed to look at the other or to ask further questions.

At last George stirred himself. 'My love,' he said, 'it is getting very late; you must go to bed,' and, lifting Jane to her feet, he went on, 'We will talk again in the morning'. He then guided a very excited but tired Jane to her room and, after a final embrace, he closed her door and went to his favourite chair in the kitchen. Here he went through the events of the evening and, like Jane, he felt that what they had planned to do was right for both of them. He had surprised himself by the ease with which he had made the proposal, but he was sure that he loved Jane and that they could make a success of the marriage and be very happy.

George was up quite early the next morning and went about preparing breakfast. Jane soon appeared looking radiant and refreshed, saying that the headache had almost completely gone. George welcomed her with a fatherly kiss, not wishing to overwhelm her so early in the morning.

'Did you really ask me to marry you, George?' she enquired with a sheepish grin. 'When I woke this morning it all seemed like a dream'.

'Yes, Jane dear,' he replied, smiling broadly. 'It was no dream; I did ask you and, what is more important, you answered yes'.

Jane could not resist the temptation to take George in her arms and hold him as she had never done before. 'Dear George,' she whispered. 'I will do all I can to make you happy'.

Just then the grandfather clock in the hall struck eight. George jumped from his chair and, with a twinkle in his eyes, he said, 'Come on, Mrs Arnold, it is time for us to be getting on board'.

George locked the door of his house and, as they walked together down the street, Jane took his arm in hers as naturally as if she had been doing it for years. George, for his part, did not feel so comfortable. How his pals would rag him if he happened to meet any of them.

When they arrived at the docks and went aboard his ship George first took Jane to his cabin, but could only stay a few minutes, after which he went up on to the bridge to direct the vessel out of the harbour and set her on course for Bideford. It was a very short voyage, but he had to make sure that they arrived at the bar — an area of shallow water where the river meets the sea — just before high tide, and then go on up the river to their moorings at the quay. George secretly hoped that none of the crew had seen Jane come aboard; but he realised he would have to tell them eventually, or at least his mate, that they were to be married.

Jane had not long to wait after the ship tied up before she stepped ashore, and she and George were able to have a chat. It was arranged that George should spend his next leave at the hotel where Jane worked. This would be in just a month and they both knew that it would seem to them to be a very long month, there was so much to be arranged, so many plans to be made. But now it was time for Jane to go home. Just a year previously a public transport had been set up between Jane's village and Bideford which travelled on two days of each week and was made up of two horses and a brake or waggonette, as it was sometimes called. After a rather formal farewell Jane set off for home, still very anxious to know if the yacht had returned safely and that her family was well, while George returned to his duties. They both knew a wonderful sense of joy in their hearts which made the future seem so bright.

It was a great relief to Jane's family and, indeed, to all the members of that little community where she lived, when she finally arrived home late that evening. There had been so much speculation as to when and how she would get home; in fact Alex

Simpson had stayed on at the hotel until he was sure that all was well with Jane. Tired as she was, there was a wonderful radiance in her face — a fact which Doctor Carter noticed and mentioned to his wife Ellen.

Everyone crowded into the hotel kitchen to hear Jane's story which she told quietly and without emotion. Then when everyone thought she had finished because there had been such a long pause she excitedly announced: 'I'm going to be married!!' There was a gasp of astonishment from the group who at first thought she was joking, but they soon learnt otherwise when Jane went on to give more details. Maria and her young sister could not understand what it all meant and burst into tears, while the older people showered Jane with congratulations.

Daniel Carter intervened at that point and suggested that Jane should go home and sleep, telling her not to come to work the next morning but to recover from her exhausting experiences. But before going to bed she had a long talk with the girls and Frank, in order to comfort them and set their minds at rest about the future. They had had a very trying time while waiting for their mother and the sudden announcement of her marriage was too much for them.

It was not long before everyone had settled

down to their normal way of life. Then, one evening soon after Jane's return, Alex Simpson was preparing to leave in his yacht on the morning tide when he met her just as she was leaving work.

'I shall be off in the morning, Jane,' he said. 'I would very much like a chat this evening if you could manage it'.

'Yes, of course,' she replied, a little taken aback. 'Where would you like to talk?'

'Why not on that lovely spot where I first saw you here,' he said. 'I won't keep you long,' as he saw a look of confusion beginning to spread across her face. 'See you at 8 o'clock then'.

It was a perfect late summer evening as they sat among the heather in the twilight, as Alex opened the conversation.

'I don't know how to begin to say what I know I should say, Jane,' he said. 'Saying I'm sorry for what happened on that trip seems so inadequate,' he went on. 'But I am truly sorry for any mistakes I made which caused you suffering'.

Jane began to feel a little as she had done when she met Alex near that same spot some two or three years before, and did not know how to answer him.

'I know that if it had not been for the storm, all would have been well,' he continued. 'Perhaps I should have thought about the possibility of a gale blowing up at this time of the year'.

Jane then surprised herself by her answer. 'There is no need for you to feel guilty,' she said. 'No-one could know such a gale could hit us. None of us want you to leave with a feeling that you have hurt us'. Then she began to blush and to look on the ground as she continued. 'Besides, see what came out of my knock on the head. I should not have met George again so soon if I had not gone in your yacht'.

Alex smiled and, putting his hand into his pocket, took out five pounds. 'Will you please accept this, Jane, as a wedding present,' he said in a husky voice. 'I hope you will be very happy'. Jane was so taken aback that she could only whisper, 'Thank you very much, you are so kind,' then, much to her surprise, she stood up and gave Alex a peck on the cheek before saying goodnight and running home, too embarrassed to talk any more.

19

The weeks up to George's visit seemed to Jane to be endless. There would be so much to talk about, so many plans to be made. Then there would be Christmas and all that that would mean to her in his company. Not long before George was due to arrive Jane had been told by Daniel Carter that there would be a vacancy in the local Coastguard Service later in the new year. This service was formed in the 1820's to look out for ships in distress on that stretch of coast which has been called a mariner's nightmare.

Jane was thrilled with this news. How wonderful it would be if George could take up such a post. With his knowledge of the sea, she thought, it might be just the kind of work he might enjoy.

At last the great day dawned and Jane could hardly contain her excitement. George was coming to the village by the new carrier service and Doctor Carter had promised to collect him from there in his pony and trap and bring him to the Quay. Jane was alone in her cottage that evening, busying herself in preparing for her visitor, when there was a tap on the door and, on opening it, she fell into George's arms a very happy woman.

Jane's cousin David had heard the wonderful news of her impending marriage to George Arnold with joy, yet also with a little apprehension. The unhappy memories of the past had not completely gone and he hoped that it would not affect their future relationship. Bill and Archie had never mentioned the events of that terrible night, even though the three men had worked together for several years since it all happened. David had seen them mature into good-living young men — now both married with small children — and faithful members of the local Methodist Church which they helped to create.

During that Christmas time Daniel Carter invited all the members of that little community to the hotel one evening to introduce George and to celebrate his and Jane's engagement. There were about a dozen families living at the Quay at that time — all working in and around the little port: lime burners, brewers, carpenters, masons, coastguards, hotel workers and those who loaded and unloaded ships and hobbled them in and out of the harbour.

All these people gave George a wonderful welcome and he, like Jane, hoped he would one day come to live amongst them. This hope took a step nearer reality when, some months later, it was agreed that he should be employed by the Coastguard Service at the end of the year.

George returned to Wales in January after having talked with Jane about their future, late into several nights. As he travelled home he began to wonder if he had not been dreaming: he found it hard to imagine himself a married man. But what he had seen and heard during his leave with Jane convinced him that he would find happiness with her and her family — they seemed to have so much in common. They had agreed that the wedding should take place at the end of September, just after George was due to retire and exactly one year after an unconscious Jane had been transferred to his ship in the Bristol Channel.

That spring and summer seemed to pass all too slowly for Jane, but it was a great help that she was kept busy at the hotel and at the doctor's surgery on three days each week, where the demand for his services had increased enormously.

The wedding was eventually held in the Parish Church when the Revd William Chanter officiated and the bells were rung by David Kellaway and his team. A wonderful reception was laid on by Daniel and Ellen Carter for the many friends and relatives. Daniel and Ellen had come to appreciate all that Jane had done for them. She had become a very popular lady since the surgery had been set up, where her caring attitude to so many people was much appreciated.

The happy couple soon settled into their new life and George was accepted and liked by all who came to know him. He often remembered that awful night when his ship was wrecked at this place where he had now come to make his home, but he determined not to allow those memories to mar the happiness of his new family and the little group of people with whom he had come to live. Life for him had completely changed, as it had for Jane. George often felt that he had been saved from the raging sea in order that he might bring to Jane a wonderful peace and joy, and this is what he dedicated himself to do.

Towards the end of that year a cloud of sadness enveloped that little community. Just after George and Jane's wedding the Revd William Chanter died after being Vicar of that parish for 62 years and had acted as Curate 10 years before that. He was a very popular priest who knew Hartland better than anyone, he had been so helpful to so many people throughout his long ministry.

Almost at the same time the owner of the Quay, Mr L W Buck, died and the Abbey and the Quay, together with the large estate, passed to his son George Stucley Buck. He was created a baronet the following year and took the name Sir George Stucley.

But the saddest event of all was the decision of Daniel and Ellen Carter to leave the Quay and live in the village. Jane was devastated when she heard this news. She had been so close to them and would miss her work at the surgery as she would have to transport. The new tenant was a man from Morwenstow, just over the border of Devon and Cornwall, called Charles Brimacombe, who remained until 1887. It was in that year that a fierce gale destroyed part of the Quay which meant the end of Hartland Quay as a trading port.

Jane was so thankful for George's support during the changes which took place at the hotel and she found it a little more difficult to settle down with the Brimacombes than she had with Doctor and Mrs Carter. But there was a lone bright spot in all this which was that her new mistress needed a young girl to look after her small daughter. Jane was not slow to suggest that Ann, her youngest child, might be given the post and this was gladly accepted by Mrs Brimacombe. Now all of Jane's family were working which made life so much more pleasant for her.

As the years passed there came the day when young Jamie, who had by this time become dedicated to his work on Mr Passmore's farm, came one evening with a very serious look on his face. When he and his mother were alone he said, 'Can I have a word with you Mum?'

Jane was taken aback, it was most unusual for Jamie to talk much. 'Yes dear,' she replied. 'What do you want to tell me?'

In a very few words the lad explained to his mother that Mr Passmore had had a long talk with him, in which he had said that as he and his wife were getting on in years and had no family of their own; it was their wish that he, Jamie, should take over the running of the farm and that it would be left to him when they died.

Jane was so surprised at what the young man — who was now 22 years old — had said that she was almost lost for words.

'Are you sure you have not made a mistake, Jamie?' she asked. 'I can't believe it's true, there must be some snag somewhere. Are you sure that you could manage that farm?'

'Yes, of course I could, mother,' the lad replied. Mr Passmore says everything is being arranged by a solicitor and the papers will be ready for signing in a few weeks'.

Jane was so excited she could hardly wait for George to come home and then to share this wonderful news with the rest of the family. Her first thought was that she should go to Mr and Mrs Passmore to thank them but thanks seemed to her to be so very inadequate at that time. It was not long before the necessary documents were completed and Farmer Hickman was duly installed, while Jane was overcome with pride and joy. She again remembered her life in that old cottage when she little thought that one day her small son would be the farmer. She felt that his father would have been so proud of him.

The new Vicar of the parish was the Revd Thomas How Chope, a young man who came with many fresh ideas which upset some people who had been used to the old fashioned ways of his predecessor for so long and who himself was destined to be the parish priest for 47 years. But David took an instant liking to his priest and was so pleased that he was able to continue his close connection with his church.

David was now living alone, his aged mother having died some two years previously. He adapted himself to being on his own quite well; the fact that he had learnt to read was a great blessing to him and, together with his hobbies of bell ringing and visiting his aged friends, life was still very full even though he himself was now reaching the age of retirement from his regular work at the Abbey.

The fact that George Arnold was now well integrated into his family and was accepted by all did not lessen the feeling of remorse that sometimes swept through David, when he remembered his past actions, even though he knew, deep down, that he had been forgiven. He sometimes toyed with the idea that he should share these thoughts with George and make a clean breast of the whole terrible episode for his sake.

He was on the point of doing this one evening when they were together when Jane came into the room. There was such a peace and joy radiating in her face that David knew that he must not go on with his plan. A picture of what it would do to her and the children was so devastating that he decided to dismiss the idea there and then for all time. He knew that his own confession had enabled him to live at peace with himself and that as a result of that terrible act his life had changed completely.

Jane's elder daughter, Maria, had been a

faithful worker at the hotel for 10 years and was liked by all who came there on holiday. She was 23 years old when her life was suddenly changed. Like her mother she, too, met a young naval officer called John Sellwood who just swept her off her feet but there was none of the embarrassment for Maria from which her mother suffered. Maria had developed into a mature young lady through her contact with so many people at the hotel.

Her mother was rather concerned at the speed with which the relationship had developed but when Maria came home one evening with the news that she was to be married the following month Jane felt that she just had to have a serious talk with her daughter.

'Are you quite sure you know what you're doing Maria?' she asked her when they were alone one evening.

'Of course I am, mother,' Maria replied confidently. 'After all I am 23 years old, you know'.

'Yes, I know that dear, but do you know enough about this young man?' Jane questioned.

'Oh, mother,' she answered. 'You're old fashioned. I love John and that's all that matters, isn't it?'

Jane did not know how to answer. This was not the quiet, shy little girl she was when she went to work at the hotel. Her mother could see something of Harry's character in her daughter.

The wedding eventually took place in the parish church where many memories, both happy and unhappy, came flooding back into Jane's mind and she was so grateful to have George's support at this time. She had the satisfaction of knowing that her daughter was starting out on married life so much better equipped in every way than she had been.

Maria's fiance and his family had stayed at the hotel for two days before the wedding and Jane had been able to observe that they were a rather different type of people to her own family and friends, but she was thankful that they seemed to accept Maria as one of their own. It was with great joy that Jane was able to see the happy couple off to their new home in Plymouth, when John was to rejoin his ship. Plymouth was a long way off in Jane's thinking and she doubted if she would see her daughter again for a long time. So she was determined to settle down with George to enjoy life in their own humble way, content with their lot and supporting each member of that little community in which they were privileged to live.

We do hope that you have enjoyed reading this large print book.

Did you know that all of our titles are available for purchase?

We publish a wide range of high quality large print books including:
**Romances, Mysteries, Classics
General Fiction
Non Fiction and Westerns**

Special interest titles available in large print are:
**The Little Oxford Dictionary
Music Book
Song Book
Hymn Book
Service Book**

Also available from us courtesy of Oxford University Press:
**Young Readers' Dictionary
(large print edition)
Young Readers' Thesaurus
(large print edition)**

For further information or a free brochure, please contact us at:
**Ulverscroft Large Print Books Ltd.,
The Green, Bradgate Road, Anstey,
Leicester, LE7 7FU, England.
Tel:** (00 44) 0116 236 4325
Fax: (00 44) 0116 234 0205

Other books in the Ulverscroft Large Print Series:

GRIANAN

Alexandra Raife

Abandoning her life in England after a broken engagement, Sally flees to Grianan, the beloved Scottish home of her childhood. Running Aunt Janey's remote country house hotel will be a complete break. Sally's brief encounter with Mike — gentle, loving but unavailable — cures the pain of her broken engagement, but leaves a deeper ache in its place. Caught up in the concerns of Grianan, Sally begins to heal. And when fate brings Mike into her life again, tragically altered, she has the strength and faith to hope that Grianan may help him too.

AN INCONSIDERATE DEATH

Betty Rowlands

In the sleepy Gloucestershire village of Marsdean, Lorraine Chant, wife of a wealthy businessman, is found strangled. But why, when both the Chants' safes had been discovered, was nothing stolen? What was Lorraine's relationship with Hugo Bayliss — a man with a dubious background and a penchant for attractive married women? How did Bayliss come to meet Sukey, police photographer and scene of crime officer, before the investigation became public? Then, in a cruel twist of fate, Sukey unwittingly plays into the hands of Lorraine's murderer . . .

THE SIMPLE LIFE

Lauren Wells

Lawrence Langland has had enough of corporate politics and fifteen-hour days. He wants out, to a simpler life. Isobel, his wife, whose gold-plated keyring says 'Born to Shop', has her own reasons for wanting to escape. Fortunately for Jacob, their eight-year-old son, it means leaving his horrible boarding school, although his elder sister Dory needs more persuading. And so the Langlands become 'downshifters', exchanging a comfortable house in suburbia for a small cottage in the countryside. Making the decision was the easy part — but can they cope with the reality?

Blair Public Library
210 S. 17th St.
Blair, Ne 68008